To Study a Long

"Delightfully civilised entertainment."

—*Sunday Telegraph*

To Study a Long Silence

V. C. Clinton-Baddeley

PERENNIAL LIBRARY
Harper & Row, Publishers
New York, Cambridge, Philadelphia, San Francisco
London, Mexico City, São Paulo, Sydney

A hardcover edition of this book was published in 1972 by Victor Gollancz Ltd., London, England. It is here reprinted by arrangement.

TO STUDY A LONG SILENCE. Copyright ©1972 by Mark Goullet. All rights reserved. Printed in the United States of America. No part of this book may be used or reproduced in any manner whatsoever without written permission except in the case of brief quotations embodied in critical articles and reviews. For information address Victor Gollancz Ltd., 14 Henrietta Street, London WC2E 8QJ, England.

First PERENNIAL LIBRARY edition published 1984.

Library of Congress Cataloging in Publication Data

Clinton-Baddeley, V. C. (Victor Clinton), 1900-1970.
    To study a long silence.

    Reprint. Originally published: London : Victor Gollancz, 1972.
    "Perennial library."
    I. Title.
[PR6053.L5T6 1984]   823'.912   83-48337
ISBN 0-06-080690-7 (pbk.)

84 85 86 87 88   10 9 8 7 6 5 4 3 2 1

I am i'th'way to study a long silence

JOHN WEBSTER, *The White Devil*

FOREWORD AND ACKNOWLEDGEMENT

To Study a Long Silence had been almost completed
by V. C. Clinton-Baddeley when he died in August 1970.

The entire plot was included in the Author's manu-
script. Descriptive passages and dialogue by his nephew,
Mark Goullet, have subsequently been incorporated into
the last two chapters.

Mr Clinton-Baddeley's executors are indebted to the
late Miss Clare Nicholl, Mr Jon Evans and Mr Ronald
Horden for valuable help.

Lines Written to be Spoken at the planting of an Oak on
Primrose Hill on April 23, 1964

'Nor marble, nor the gilded monuments
Of Princes, shall outlive this powerful rhyme'—
The boast was courtly, but (as happened) true:
Your lightest words, good sir, yield not to Time.

The marble's chipped, the gold is smeared with grey,
The broken canopy conceals the bone,
Yours, surely, was a modest claim, good sir:
An English oak lasts longer than the stone.

The oak that sheltered Edward's Parliament;
The Abbot's tree; the Reformation Oak;
That ancient tree from which Glendower watched
While Harry Hotspur fought with Bolingbroke.

All these were old when you were born, good sir—
And live, great oaks from Saxon acorns sprung;
And even now, new-green in Arden stand
Oaks that were inches-high when you were young.

An oak, 'unwedgeable' (your word, good sir)
Is liker you than any mason's skill:
And so, our tribute on this famous day,
We plant an oak upon this famous hill.

Recklessly once you said your words would last
'So long as men can breathe or eye can see'—
Lend us a little of your humour, sir,
That just so long may last this English tree.

V. C. C.-B.

CONTENTS

PART ONE

THE COMEDY

RETURNING TO THE bedroom from the kitchen, Harriet Bastable looked first at their disordered bed, and then at the bathroom door. Judging by the splashing Alan would be safely engaged for some minutes.

She crossed the room and sat down at the dressing-table. What she saw in the looking-glass was infinitely pleasing. She loved the way her earrings glowed against her dark hair, and the way the hair billowed to her shoulders.

There was a ring on the table with a large red stone. Harriet picked it up and held it near her eyes. Then she drew it on her finger, and stretched her arm out, admiring the stone at a distance. Then she placed her hand in a dramatic pose on the green kimono wrapped across her bosom. She loved that ring: but what she really loved was herself wearing it.

A minute later, when the bathroom door opened suddenly behind her, she was surprised. Quickly she lowered her hand: but not quickly enough. Alan Bastable had seen the picture in the looking-glass.

'I told you to leave it alone,' he said, striding forward, angrily dropping his towel behind him.

'I was only trying it on.'

'You've done that before. Take it off.'

'All right,' said Harriet. 'But I don't see why you have to make such a scene.'

'It's my ring, that's why,' said Alan, slipping it on his finger.

'If you value it so much why don't you get it insured?'

'I don't want it insured. It's not worth insuring. I value it for sentimental reasons. Are your earrings insured?'

'No—but—'

' "No—but" for my ring too. I can't afford it.'

'You're a great fool.'

'I can't afford it. I can't afford anything.'

'A year ago, when you had the face to marry me—'

'A year ago I thought I would have some money. You know why. It wasn't my fault that I didn't get it.'

'Anyone but you would have found out before marrying. Heir to somebody's annuity! You're an entire fool.'

'Money, money, money! You think of nothing else.'

She could not fail to admire him. He was wearing nothing but a ring, and it suited him even better than it had suited her. But that did not alter the fact that she hated him.

'You promised me money—and you promised me love.'

'Well?'

'Don't say "Well",' said Harriet, suddenly getting up and retreating towards the kitchen. 'You know very well what I mean.' Dramatically she turned round in the doorway. 'You're not only a pauper, you're a lecher.'

'You ought to go on the stage,' said Alan Bastable.

Harriet slammed the door.

'Buck up and make the coffee,' shouted Alan, winding himself into his towel.

On the other side of the door Harriet dropped a cup into the sink.

It was the beginning of another day.

Five minutes later, drinking coffee in the kitchen, Alan said, 'When are you called?' He did not look up from the newspaper.

'There's a rehearsal at ten,' said Harriet.

'I don't have to go in till the afternoon. You can have the car.'

'Thanks.'

It was some sort of an accommodation.

When Harriet had gone Alan Bastable returned to the

bedroom with the paper. There was no need to dress before noon. He climbed back into bed.

The paper was a bore. That did not occupy him long. Then he lay back and gazed at the ceiling. There was a stain in the far right corner which had been there as long as he had known the place. Somebody's bath water presumably. No one had ever attempted to put it right. Alan Bastable rather liked it. You could make it into anything—a continent, an island, a pre-historic bird, a face. At the moment it was the face of doom. And yes, he thought, Derek Wynter would have to help. Yes, some time that afternoon he would pay a call on Derek Wynter. Derek had been helpful before. He must be helpful again.

In the end he got up at eleven. There were letters on the carpet in the hall. Two bills and a fat packet posted abroad. Inside the packet were brightly coloured brochures, offering a treasure house of books, a dynamic album of gramophone records, and, best of all, at no extra charge, an eastern army choir, singing "Birch Trees", "Gentle Anna", "Gaily the Friendly Tanks Roll By", "Hark to the Kremlin Bells" and similar favourites, a delicious bonus record for all those signing this advantageous order form.

'This unique offer can never be repeated,' said the circular.

'Well, that's something,' said Alan Bastable, and dropped the lot in the waste-paper basket.

It was half past twelve when he left the flat. It was only a fifteen minute bus drive to Winston Manor.

II

'Do come,' Mr Pomeroy had written in reply to Dr Davie's letter. 'The performance is at seven-thirty, but come earlier if you can. I'd be delighted to show you the school. There will be tea at four. I think there may be a rehearsal. Get off the bus at the Green Dragon—go down Merton Road, and there you are.'

And, at about five to four, there he was, in the midst of northern suburbia, regarding with pleasure a house which had once been in the country. Even now it was enclosed in a garden and circled by an eighteenth-century wall. London had flowed towards Winston Manor like a flood, had hesitated at the gate, and then passed by on either side, ensuring for the tenants of the neo-Georgian houses in Faber Road and Winston Crescent the contemplation of a glorious dark red wall, topped in springtime with lilac and laburnum. Beyond the wall were larger trees, plane, chestnut, and cedar. At one point a tulip tree filled the sky, old as the house and nearly as wide.

Merton Road, just round the corner, is quite different. Those are late Victorian houses with grand dingy steps to front doors no longer dignified, their pillars scrawled with enormously boring information such as "West Ham Will Fight Again" or with more debatable opinions, as "Amy Farrant is a twit" or "Leslie Moon is a Fairy". "Joan is . . ." "Arthur is . . ." These scribblers are always so positive, thought Dr Davie. I wish I were half as sure of anything.

There was nothing of that kind in Faber Road and Winston Crescent. The old red wall was far too rough to harbour such indignities. And indeed the residents owed much to the house, much to that wall, much to the garden; and, perhaps because subconsciously they recognized the fact, they showed no hostility towards the mixed crowd of young people who passed through its gates in beards and beads, in mini-skirts and maxicoats. It was not only the Green Dragon that benefited. It was generally felt that something had been added to the neighbourhood by the Winston School of Dramatic Art. Indeed several of the residents were a little proud of this friendly involvement with the Muses, and very gladly visited the school theatre to see the public performances.

There was to be such an occasion this evening. Davie paused a moment to read the notice on the gate.

Third Year Students
present
Il Pellegrino Fido Amante
a *commedia dell'arte* play
directed by
Tito Adriano

Tonight was the second and last performance. The *commedia dell'arte* was Dr Davie's hobby: of course he had wanted to come. Masks—you don't see them every day.

Trees in the drive were turning a November red. And deep red was the old square house, built in the reign of William and Mary. Over the front door were two plaques commemorating former owners. Sir William Button, Admiral, 1772/1840; and Dame Edith Pinn, 1865/1941. Davie conceived an immediate liking for the admiral. He could see him pacing the quarter-deck, a telescope tucked under his arm: jolly with the midshipmen: greatly beloved by the men. But there was something forbidding about that other one. No one, he was sure, had ever accused Dame Edith of being a twit. He suspected a dedicated interference in other people's affairs, a life-time's bossing of committee meetings.

There was no one about, but the front door stood open. Dr Davie stepped inside. On his left was a big board covered with notices and time-tables, on his right a table bearing a bowl of flowers and a card inviting visitors to walk upstairs to the office. As he went, he commended the noble curve of the staircase and the admirable banisters. Here good Sir William had laid his honest palm—how odd that was, thought Dr Davie: hands across the oak with Sir William Button. And also, he was obliged to concede, also with Dame Edith Pinn.

From somewhere down a corridor came the sound of a

soprano singing scales—the top note like a stab in the back. Good God! How very regrettable, said Dr Davie to himself.

Then he crossed the landing and knocked on the door marked "Enquiries".

III

'Oh, yes,' said Miss Pringle. 'Mr Pomeroy is expecting you, Dr Davie. He's just gone down to the theatre, but he won't be long. He said I was to take you to his room. It's this way.'

'Thank you.'

'I'm sure he won't be more than a minute,' said Miss Pringle, opening the door next to her own. 'Please take a seat.'

'Thank you,' Davie said again—but, left alone, he rejected the seat and crossed the room to the window.

Immediately opposite was the drive. To the left was a lawn and a path leading towards a large round modern building which was doubtless the theatre. Oho! The Winston School was clearly up to date. A round theatre boded "theatre in the round". None of your antiquated prosceniums. Yes—but that also meant none of your cupids brandishing torches, none of your golden young men playing lyres, no glittering curtain, no gilt, no plush. And Davie loved all those things. But then, he was forced to remember, there had been no plush, no glittering curtain, in ancient Athens—and he was a Greek scholar. A Greek scholar in love with the eighteenth century. Everything is good, he agreed with himself, provided only that it is well done. And having thus braced himself to accept the Winston Theatre, Dr Davie turned about and surveyed Mr Pomeroy's office.

It was a fine square room, perhaps in other days the principal bedroom of Winston Manor. In here, maybe, Sir William Button . . .

In the centre of the room, on Mr Pomeroy's ample table,

three shining objects reflected the last of the sun. Instead of ugly In and Out trays there were two neat groups of papers to left and right of the table, secured by large glass paperweights. He did hesitate a moment: he knew it was not quite good manners: but he could never resist these things. He loved the feel of their smooth round tops, their colours, their symmetry, and their satisfactory heaviness. He had to pick them up and examine them. They were beauties.

The third shining thing on Mr Pomeroy's table was a large silver frame, containing the picture of a woman and two small children, one of each sort. Davie was suspicious about wives in silver frames. Why did so many men who sit in offices feel obliged to stare all day at a picture of their family? Surely it was not because they were likely to forget how they looked. Surely it was not because they could not bear to be parted from them. Surely it was not because they needed that sort of check on their libidinous natures—the silent reproof of all those trusting eyes. If not for love and not for prudence, it could only be because the picture was a form of discreet insurance—it pleased the person in the frame. Or, was it only because it was the done thing, like having a rolled umbrella in the stand in the corner?

I am not a cynic, said Davie to himself. I just see things as I feel they are. If I were Mr Pomeroy I would not willingly endure that picture frame. Especially with all these rival entertainments.

From frames on the walls young faces smiled down at him—yours ever Bill and affectionately Christine—all of them earnestly inviting some nice theatrical engagement, and some inviting who knows what beside.

Dr Davie submitted the gallery to close scrutiny. Then he sat down on the chair near the table—which was what Miss Pringle had suggested he should do in the first place.

'Goodness!' said Dr Davie.

And that was when the door opened and Mr Pomeroy came

in, voluble, amiable, and apologetic. And not much over forty, Davie thought. He was wearing a green tie with a fawn suit, which was just the sort of vanity Dr Davie approved.

IV

'In the dear dead days,' said Davie, setting his cup down on the trolley table, which Miss Pringle had wheeled into the room in the wake of Mr Pomeroy: 'in the dear dead days, when the theatre was theatrical, people "went on the stage" as they might run away to sea, or follow the gold rush. Salaries might be bad, prospects imaginary—but Hope sprang eternal in the actor's breast. He had a voice, a face, a figure, and an ardent desire to display all three. The fact that he had no training was entirely insignificant. He got his training as he went along, and if he had the temperament, as Nicholas Nickleby or Henry Irving had it (the one is quite as credible a character as the other), he prospered.'

'I agree,' said Mr Pomeroy. 'That was the best school of acting: it was the school of practice. But the point is that the old theatre no longer exists. The provincial houses have degenerated into Bingo halls, and touring companies are gone with the theatrical landlady.'

'The theatre diminishes,' said Davie. 'I see that. But it appears that the number of young people convinced that they have a singular theatrical gift does not diminish. Nor does the number of acting schools. Can you teach a man to act?'

Mr Pomeroy smiled in a rather embarrassed way, as though he had been detected in some dishonesty.

'Well—no—' he said, 'you can't. I agree. Because the real things that make an actor—wit, personality, perception, and a good ear—are not to be learnt from anyone's instruction. An actor may learn to fence or to sing, but the best part of his art is inborn.'

22

'Exactly.'

'But the schools do act as a sieve. The uncomprehending, the inaudible, the dull, the tone-deaf, the lunatic fringe (and there are all these) slip through the mesh, are somehow persuaded to devote their talents to something less demanding: and what's left can be given an opportunity to practise its trade. That is the chief point in a school. It gives the actor a chance to act. That's good, isn't it?'

'Certainly it is. Touring with Irving they usually spent years waving a banner.'

Mr Pomeroy leaned forward and offered Davie a cigarette.

'No thank you,' said Davie, 'I have a belief in the prophetic wisdom of doctors.'

Mr Pomeroy put his case back in his pocket. 'This *commedia dell'arte* stuff you're interested in,' he said, 'now that's something you *can* teach. Because they none of them know anything about it. It's a traditional art. They've got to learn how to play it. And our Tito Adriano knows all about it. *Lazzos.* How are you on your *lazzos*, Dr Davie?'

'Reasonably well, I think. *Lazzos* are fundamental stage jokes—just as funny now as they always have been: but they need superb timing. I remember an old English music hall comedian who used to sit on a deck chair which always collapsed. One knew it would collapse, but every time it did collapse the joke was new made. That was straight descended from the old Italian comedy. And all those japes about thinking you've lost one of your feet, just because you can't see it: or conceiving the alarming idea that you have suddenly acquired four hands: and the magnificent nonsense of the Doctor's conversation: and all the impudence of Harlequin: these are jokes of the sweetest simplicity, but they're monumentally difficult to play. It's speed, it's timing, it's bubbling good humour.'

'And the performance is never exactly the same—and that's so good for our actors. The show is all worked out on an agreed scenario, but within those limits they can improvise. That's essential—and it's traditional.'

'I'm a sucker for those gorgeous half-masks,' said Davie. 'I trust you have masks for Harlequin and Pantaloon and the Doctor—'

'Indeed we have,' said Mr Pomeroy. 'Glorious ones—come and see. I think there's a very late rehearsal going on for tonight's show. It might interest you.'

'Certainly it would.'

'Then come on,' said Mr Pomeroy, suddenly rising and leading the way to the door, but he paused as suddenly on the landing with, 'Sorry! I must have two words with Miss Pringle—I won't keep you half a minute,' and disappeared into the office like a shot. Mr Pomeroy was a precipitate person.

Davie waited. It was only half past four, but the long window behind the stairs framed an inky sky, and as no one had thought to put the landing light on, he stood there in the shadows. So quiet it was, for a moment he half expected to see some Regency maiden climbing the stairs with a trimmed lamp, or old Sir William, candlestick in hand, stumping across the landing. Instead, the present declared its own events. A door swung open on the far side of the landing and a rectangle of artificial light fell across the carpet. To Davie the figure that came quickly out of the room was at first a silhouette, then, as it turned towards the head of the stairs, the light falling on its back, a general impression of bead necklaces, a cowboy jacket, and a head of auburn hair. Its feet clattered down the stairs and faded into silence.

It was the other man, the man in the room, who held Davie's eyes. Full in the light, he stood behind a table covered in papers—quite still and staring through the open door at the patch of light on the dark floor. It was as troubled a face as Davie had ever seen.

And then the office door opened and Mr Pomeroy came

24

out, and the man inside the room stepped out of sight and shut the door.

'Sorry to keep you,' said Mr Pomeroy.

As he turned towards the stairs Davie noticed the word Bursar painted on the door across the landing. Underneath it was a name: but he could not read that.

v

'It's a busy life,' said Mr Pomeroy as he went downstairs.

'With its own drama, no doubt,' said Davie.

'One glorious round of drama! If it isn't time-tables it's grants: if it isn't grants it's students' love affairs. Miss Pringle looks after the time-tables—that's high comedy of course: the bursar looks after the grants—that's a social drama: and I look after the love affairs, which is pure French farce.'

It was lighter in the garden. They turned down the path towards the theatre. Halfway along the path on the left was a long low wooden building. 'This is the gym,' said Mr Pomeroy, opening the door. 'Nothing on at the moment. It's used for limbering and movement classes.'

'Nice,' said Davie, peering inside. 'So you teach them how to move,' he added, as they walked on down the path. 'One wonders how the old actors got on without movement classes.'

'We don't know, do we? My guess is that some of them were pretty starchy, pretty selfish and considerably unco-operative. Movement is a twentieth century notion. I think it's a good one.'

Siddons, Kean, Macready, Irving, Martin Harvey: it was a different tradition. 'I don't really know what a movement class is,' Davie admitted. 'But I'm sure you're right.'

They had reached a side entrance to the theatre, and 'Here we are,' said Mr Pomeroy, opening a door and leading Davie into a corridor. 'This is the heart of the matter. New, as you can see. The apple of our eyes. As well as the theatre there's a rehearsal studio, a fair number of dressing-rooms, a scenery studio, and a wardrobe. We thought it a good idea to get them all under one roof. This is the wardrobe.

'School wardrobes are pretty tatty of course,' said Mr Pomeroy, pausing, hand on door knob. 'Naturally we can't have lots of new clothes, and we can't have teams of seam-stresses constantly repairing things. Between you and me that's one of the reasons for modern dress productions. They do *look* well. A seventeenth century play in shabby clothes and scruffy wigs just looks as though one hasn't tried. But a modern dress production looks as though one has done it on purpose.'

'That's a very wise remark,' said Davie—and noted privately that the Director of the Winston School was rather good value.

'We've got a marvellous wardrobe mistress,' said Mr Pomeroy. 'But it's a struggle. Come on in.'

Rows and rows of clothes on hangers made avenues across the room, all neatly arranged like a history of England, from Constance to Lady Bracknell, from codpiece to sponge-bag trousers.

At the end of the central alley, back to the window, a small determined-looking woman stood brandishing an electric iron.

'Hullo Mrs Goode,' said Mr Pomeroy. 'May we enter?'

At the Winston School it was customary, as Davie presently observed, to call everyone by their Christian names. The one exception was Mrs Goode, who looked so matriarchal that no one had ever wanted to try it on. Nor indeed would it have been possible, for no one had ever discovered what her name was. The truth was that Mrs Goode's parents in a moment of operatic enthusiasm had called her Semiramis, and Mrs Goode was understandably coy about it. For her own part, she called everyone "dear" and seemed to mean it. She was the heart of kindness—and also the soul of justice: no student was ever favoured above another in her department. So 'Hallo Mrs Goode,' said Mr Pomeroy. 'May we come in? This is Dr Davie. I'm showing him round.'

'How d'you do?' said Davie.

Mrs Goode's answer was perhaps routine, but to a newcomer it was refreshing.

'I really don't know,' said Mrs Goode, shaking like a jelly at her own repartee. 'But we do do it somehow, don't we, dear?'

'You do indeed,' said Mr Pomeroy. 'How is it this time? Have you seen the show?'

'Well, yes, I did, dear, though I shouldn't have spared the time," said Mrs Goode thumping her iron down on an eighteenth century corsage. 'I'm far too busy with the next thing. Mrs Candour has always been played fat and well you know it. And now you've cast Jackie Marsden for the part, and she's as thin as a rake and everything has to be taken in. But I did see the show last night, dear, and they've got everything—as you can see from the rack.'

She pointed to a gap among the hangers. At the end of the rack there were still a few dresses—a girl's gay frock, a crimson cloak and tights, a sombre black doublet and lawyer's gown.

'Aren't those *commedia* costumes too?' asked Davie.

'Yes, dear—Columbine, Pantaloon, the Doctor. We've got several of them. Have to with this lot, dear, or I'd be up all night mending.'

'And there's a mask,' said Davie.

'The Doctor, dear.'

'How glorious! Do put it on.'

Pomeroy picked up the mask and slipped it over his ears.

'Pomeroy, thou art translated!' said Davie. 'It's so good—those critical eyebrows, and that monstrous, superior nose! You'd think the thing would have no life. But put it on and it seems able to alter its expression. I suppose it's a trick of the light: it changes with every movement and literally does alter the expression.'

'I think the point is that the mask doesn't carry it alone.'

Beneath that interfering nose the lips and chin of Mr Pomeroy were moving, but it did not seem to be Mr Pomeroy who spoke. It was the Doctor.

'You do have to be an actor,' he said. 'It's no use just standing: you have to *do* something intelligent with your face inside the mask. The mask doubles the actor. There's a man within and a man without. When I do this,' said Mr Pomeroy, making a series of dramatic gestures, 'it's not just the mask and a costume on a stick. It's me, too, giving a performance as the Doctor.'

'I perceive you are a bit of an actor yourself,' said Davie.

'I should be,' said Pomeroy, taking off the mask. 'I battered my head against the stage doors of a good many theatres before I took up with this lark. But come on Dr Davie: we must be getting along. Goodbye Mrs Goode.'

"Goodbye, dear,' said Mrs Goode, waving a cheerful hand. 'You'd make a lovely Doctor, dear, with your legs.'

'We couldn't exist without that old girl,' said Edward Pomeroy as he shut the wardrobe door. 'Her parents were on the stage: she was quite a good provincial actress herself: I saw her once in one of those Shakespeare touring companies which don't exist any longer. She was doing Lady Macbeth and Portia.'

'Crime and Punishment. Was she any good?'

'To a schoolboy, yes. Her grand-daughter is one of our third year students—Mrs Goode's peculiar pride, treasure and anxiety. You'll see her tonight. And you'll probably see Mrs Goode too. Whatever she says about being busy she's always there. Now I'll take you to the auditorium.'

The corridor, like the building, was circular. It passed round the back of the stage. 'Dressing-rooms on this side, the stage on that,' said Pomeroy. 'In its humble way it's like the opera house at Vienna. That door takes you to the O.P. side of the stage, and, just round the curve—here you are—this one takes you to the Prompt side.'

'I'm glad you keep the old names,' said Davie.

'Oh yes—I'm all in favour of tradition, provided it doesn't interfere with the present. But, mark you, this doesn't mean we use a prompter.'

'I bet you don't,' said Davie. 'Likewise you've got a box office but no boxes.'

'And curtain calls but no curtain,' said Mr Pomeroy. 'That's the canteen on the left.'

At the end of the corridor a door opened on to the foyer. Pomeroy led Davie to one of the auditorium doors.

'Here we are,' he said. 'I'm afraid I'll have to leave you now. Take a seat inside and watch as much as you like: but they can't go on much longer. The canteen's open at six—but my advice is to go along to the Green Dragon. They do quite a decent dinner there. I won't say goodbye: I'll hope to see you in the interval or after the show.'

'It's been very good of you to take so much trouble,' said Davie.

'Not a bit,' said Mr Pomeroy.

Davie opened the door and slipped inside. He was at the back of the auditorium. For a few seconds all he could see was the stage, a pool of light in the darkness. When the theatre took shape he sat down on the nearest seat on the gangway. It was a small house, and the floor was well raked.

On the far side of the house, some six rows from the back, a girl sat so deeply sunk in her seat that she was invisible except for her head of black hair, and that was dark against dark.

Sitting in the front row a man was talking to the actors. He was a great gesticulator and Davie guessed that he was Tito Adriano.

On stage were four men and a girl. The girl was wearing a pink and blue ribboned dress. She was probably Columbine. One of the men was wearing a black gown and a half-mask with a long nose: and there it was again, *il Dottore*, the Doctor, the learned man from Bologna who talks such exemplary nonsense. Davie was delighted. Two other men were in ordinary clothes. Perhaps they were Harlequin and the Captain, the beautiful fire-eating soldier of fortune. The fourth man was not in costume either, but he held in his hand a distinguishing feature—the mask of Pantaloon. Wearing that mask—whatever his clothes—he would miraculously become Pantaloon. Without that mask he was just another young man with a good-looking but bad-tempered face, his auburn hair well brushed and fringed like a Plantagenet squire. He looked older than the others. Round his neck hung several necklaces. He wore a skin jacket, studded, and with white lamb's wool on it. He was certainly a memorable figure. And Davie did in fact remember him.

It did not look as though Davie was going to see any rehearsing. The director was giving notes, and chiefly addressing himself to the three men. Certainly Columbine felt free to think of other matters. Her hand was lightly linked with Pantaloon's: and once she lifted it up and played with the ring on his finger, a chunk of shining theatrical jewellery fit for some villain duke in a Renaissance play. She slipped it off and tried it on herself, but Pantaloon, without withdrawing his eyes from Tito Adriano, took it away from her. He was cross: but not with Columbine.

'All right, Tito,' said the man who was Pantaloon. 'We've *got* all that. Now for God's sake let's pack it in. It's gone six o'clock.'

'Sorry,' said Tito Adriano. 'I didn't realize. Let's break. Good luck.'

'And about time,' said Pantaloon moving away.

'You were late, Alan,' said the Doctor incautiously, his prodigious nose giving the words a sanctimonious flavour which Pantaloon was in no mood to accept.

'Oh—for God's sake!' he shouted, and disappeared into the wings.

There appeared to be a little edginess on stage.

The actors gone, Tito Adriano collected some papers and stuffed them in his brief-case. He was walking towards a side exit from the auditorium when the girl with the dark hair leant forward.

'Tito.'

She had made no effort to be heard, but it was a stage-trained voice and Tito Adriano heard her.

'Harriet! I didn't know you were there.'

Her long black hair was caught back at the sides by a red velvet fillet, and a red stone shone at the lobe of her ear.

'You might have guessed,' said Harriet, stepping down the gangway.

'I suppose I might have,' said Adriano. Then he touched her arm and said, 'Does Alan know you're here?'

'I've no idea,' said Harriet, 'and really I don't care.'

'Then come back to the flat. There's time. I can give you some dinner.'

Davie had sat in the darkness like a mouse, not because he wanted to overhear, but because he did not want the embarrassment of discovery. He saw Adriano's outstretched hand. He saw how freely and easily Harriet placed her hand in his. And he sat like a mouse and waited till Tito Adriano and his lady friend had gone.

Then he too got up, and left the theatre by the way he had come in.

Two minutes later he was on his way to the Green Dragon, pondering, as he went, how strangely human relationships may force themselves on the attention. He had sought for nothing, but he now knew, for what it was worth, that Tito Adriano was very much "in" with the girl with the dark hair; that Alan was "out"; that Alan (but was it the same Alan?) was a cantankerous actor; that Alan was Pantaloon.

And he also knew that it had been Alan whom he had seen earlier that evening, from across the dark landing, leaving the bursar's room.

It seemed there was a combination here of two of Mr Pomeroy's daily problems—the French farces and the social dramas.

VI

The light from the street lamp fell full on the crumbling porticos of Merton Road, illuminating the inscriptions on the dirty paint. It was odd, thought Davie, how long such *graffiti* lingered. On this decayed property no one was likely to wipe them out and there they might remain for years. Indeed, Amy Farrant, rebutting the charge of twit, might already have become a trusted secretary, and Leslie Moon no fairy but the disenchanted father of two poisonous little girls. If those remarks had been scrawled on a pillar in the forum at Rome someone would have written a monstrous great book about them. And it would not have been true. History is a delusion, thought Davie. We can never know enough about anyone. And when one has to cope with propagandists reporting Richard III as a murderer and Amy Farrant as a twit, one's whole vision is disturbed. 'Great is the truth and will prevail.' But surely it often does not.

The Green Dragon occupied the corner site at the end of Merton Road. It was new, but its owners had deliberately striven to establish a Pickwickian reputation. The walls bore coloured prints of coaches and horses. There was a hunting horn in the hall. A fox's mask inappropriately adorned the bar. And, if ever the age of machines should come to an end, and farmers should turn again to the patient horse, the Green Dragon would be amply provided to supply the necessary brass trimmings. The walls of the bar and the dining-room were hung with these trophies. They twinkled in the light, and were, Davie admitted, rather pretty. But he guessed that they had never seen the inside of a farm stable. They were newly antique, new as the old world settle by the electric log fire. Still, don't let's be critical, thought Davie. It's warm, and not unpleasing.

He collected a whisky and water. Then he sat down on the settle, and considered the menu. There was tomato soup: there was a mixed grill: there was a fruit salad. That was not bad, and he agreed to have it.

While he waited there was also an evening paper which someone had left on a stool. Davie took it into the dining-room. The national crisis, he observed, was as acute as ever. Passionately the journalists strove to make that clear. The public had to be daily astonished by that revelation, outraged by this one, comforted, nevertheless, by this piece of cockney humour, and purged by sorrow for some small child's predicament. There was not a string that someone had not attempted to twang. And then there were the sports pages. Someone had kicked a penalty goal. Better, someone had kicked the referee. This was news for which the people of Britain were avidly waiting.

Ultimately, and inevitably, the public was obliged to turn, whatever its secret doubts, to see what Ulrica had to say about the influence of the stars upon the morrow. Davie was Gemini. Solemnly he consulted his fate.

For him, and about ten million other members of the clan, Ulrica had grave words. 'Avoid financial dealings till the afternoon,' she urged. 'Difficulties with partners may be experienced but later in the evening an unexpected encounter with a stranger should prove to be mutually satisfactory.' Ten million Gemini fated to meet ten million strangers, and all satisfactorily! It sounded a prolific night's work. For his part—but speculation about his own prospects in this frolic was diverted by the arrival of the soup. Dr Davie settled himself down behind a meagre vase of plastic daffodils born out of due time, folded up the newspaper, unfolded his paper napkin, and dipped his spoon into that orange-vermilion liquid universally accepted as cream of tomato. It was hot. In its own way it was good.

33

VII

In the wake of the fruit salad a young man wearing jeans entered the dining-room and crossed the floor to Davie's table.

'Are you Dr Davie?' he asked.

'Yes, I am.'

'Edward asked me to see that you were all right.'

'Edward?'

'Edward Pomeroy.'

Davie had always attempted to keep abreast with the times, but this dedicated pre-occupation with Christian names was something he found acutely difficult to accept. Was there to be no distinguishing between friends and acquaintances, between acquaintances and persons? Mr Pomeroy could be nothing but Pomeroy to him, and here he was being forced to be matey about Edward to a third party he'd never met before. It reminded him of the ghastly insincerity of B.B.C. disc jockeys. But, as there was nothing to be done about it, he said, 'Yes, thank you: I'm doing myself very well. Have a glass of something with me, will you? And tell me who you are.'

'Thanks,' said the young man, sitting down beside him with unaffected grace. 'I'm Martin Searle and I'd like a glass of lager, thank you very much'—which was just the sort of straight answer that Davie always enjoyed. Martin Searle was fair and slim, topped with a mop of hair, which was tousled, but in an orderly manner. Below the hair was an enormous smile. In spite of the reference to Edward, Davie voted in favour of Mr Searle.

'What's your place in this galley?' he asked.

'I'm a second-year student and in tonight's show I'm a sort of all purpose understudy to all the male characters. The whole thing, you know, is based on improvisation and no performance is ever exactly the same as the last one. So it wouldn't be too diffi-cult for me to waltz in and play any of the parts if I had to.'

34

'At a minute's notice?'

'At no notice at all. It's part of the training.'

'It's part of the tradition, too. Coming down to see this *commedia* thing, my mind's rather full of that—but I suppose this is only a side-show really. You do lots of other things, don't you.'

'Oh yes—with other directors. Tito's only here certain days. The rest of his time he directs things at Renton's.'

'Another school?'

'Yes. Not like this one. As far as I can understand all they do there is fencing and acting.'

'Just *plain acting*?'

'Yes.'

'Like Mrs Siddons?'

'I believe so.'

'Actually using the author's words?'

'Yes.'

'You astound me,' said Davie. 'But they do employ Tito Adriano?'

'Yes. The bloke in charge is rather keen on the *commedia*. If we're going to improvise anything, for God's sake let's improvise that, he's reported to have said.'

'I think,' said Davie, 'that I rather approve of him, whoever he is.'

'Renton, I suppose.'

'That's a very rash assumption,' said Davie. 'What's the time?'

'Seven o'clock.'

Davie put a hand out for his coat. 'I should move.'

'There's plenty of time. But you would like a cup of coffee in the canteen. It's better there.'

'All right. Conduct me thither,' said Davie, getting up.

So Davie paid his bill and the two of them walked down Merton Road towards the school.

Presently Davie said, 'Tell me who Harriet is.'

35

Martin Searle turned his head and looked hard at Davie before replying, 'Harriet is Alan Bastable's wife.'

'That is rather a small answer. Who is Alan Bastable?'

'He's one of the third-year students. You'll see him tonight. He plays Pantaloon.'

'*That* Alan.' (So it was the same Alan.) 'Then I've seen him already. But not acting . . . I had rather gathered the impression that Harriet was carrying on with Tito Adriano.'

'And you're so right,' said Martin Searle.

'What does Alan Bastable say to that?'

'Nothing. He's largely to blame. *He*'s left *her* to go chasing after another of our girls.'

'Ah—and is the pursuit successful?'

'I hope not,' said Searle. 'Laura's much too good for him.'

This time it was Davie who turned his head. He summed up young Mr Searle by lamplight. It was not, he thought, a very difficult calculation.

And now there was no easy way to a change of conversation. Davie and Searle walked up the drive in silence till they reached the turning to the theatre. Then, 'The canteen's at the back,' said Martin. 'Mind how you go. This part of the paving isn't finished yet. Are you all right?'

'Thanks. I can see.'

'And this is it,' said Martin Searle, opening a door. Across the corridor were wide double doors, each with a round window. Beyond the window were lights and heads, and two shining urns.

'Are you coming in?' asked Davie.

Instead of answering, Martin Searle stood for two seconds surveying the scene. Then he turned to Davie and said, with a certain confusion, 'No—if you don't mind, I think I won't. That is, if you can manage all right. I don't want to—'

'You run along,' said Davie. 'I can manage perfectly. See you later on, maybe. Or even on the stage perhaps?'

'You wouldn't recognize me if you did,' said Martin. 'Goodbye.'

Before entering the canteen Davie also looked through the round window. There were about twenty young people there. And gracious, he thought, I'm sadly under-dressed. What will they think of me? I've not even got a necklace.

Then, standing in a corner, he noticed, as Martin Searle had noticed a few seconds earlier, the arrogant young man who was called Alan, who played Pantaloon, who was married to Harriet, who was chasing Laura. He was talking to a wonderfully pretty young woman. And, Davie guessed, a fairly stupid one. From the rapt expression on her face, anyone would have thought that Alan Bastable was Apollo himself. It was the girl that Davie had seen on the stage earlier in the evening—and he guessed that she was Laura.

Davie pushed open the door and went in. And almost simultaneously Alan Bastable advanced to the other door and went out with the girl in tow. It was eight minutes past seven and Davie wondered a little why he had been there. He did not know that it was rather a thing with Alan Bastable to be just late enough to agitate the stage manager and all the other performers.

Davie went up to the counter and asked for a cup of coffee. And, a little further down the corridor, Alan Bastable deposited the girl in her dressing room with a parting kiss on the tip of her nose, and then strolled on to his own room, which he shared with Michael Teed, who played the Captain. It was ten past seven. He was perfectly safe. Wearing a half-mask he did not have to make his face up. He could dress in five minutes. There was nothing to get scatty about. He knew exactly what he was doing. But he was not behaving in a professional manner. That was something the Winston School of Dramatic Art had failed to instil into Alan Bastable.

'All ready, I see,' he said. 'I trust you know your lines.' But Michael Teed was not fool enough to answer that kind of remark. He said, 'Edward says there's a chap in front who knows about the *commedia*.'

'There's a damn sight too many people who know all about

everything,' said Alan Bastable. 'I wish they'd just sit in the audience and enjoy themselves.'

'That's up to us,' said Michael Teed. 'Prepare to be witty.'

'I don't have to be witty,' said Bastable, picking up his mask. 'Not with a nose like this.'

VIII

At ten past seven Edward Pomeroy was having a word with Miss Pringle up at the house.

'Are you coming tonight, Priscilla?'

'I can't, Edward, I just can't. There are all those audition forms to sort out. There are a hundred and forty-six applications—'

'God's truth!'

'Of which a hundred are reasonable.'

'How appalling! Sixty of them will be wasting their time.'

'But you've *got* to hear them all, Edward.'

The Christian name lark did not sit very happily on Miss Pringle. But she knew it was the expected thing and had made it a sort of responsibility to get it right: with the result that she used the name Edward twice as often as she would ever have used the words Mr Pomeroy.

'You've got to hear them, Edward,' she repeated. 'And it will take—let's see—ten times a hundred divided by sixty—that's sixteen hours.'

'No!'

'Yes, it is. And that means four consecutive mornings. It's only once a year, Edward. Now do run along. You'll be late for the show if you don't go at once.'

'I suppose I better had.'

'This won't take me long. Forty-six non-starters. And a hundred sets of instructions,' said Miss Pringle cheerfully, and she sat down firmly at her desk. 'I might see the end of the show after all.'

A wonderful woman. As Pomeroy went down the stairs he could hear the busy clatter of the typewriter and the ping of the little bell. Up against it, Miss Pringle was in her element.

IX

Tito Adriano's flat in Amelia Gardens had been constructed with much ingenious sub-division from the first floor rooms of a large Victorian mansion. In the years to come it would perhaps be described by an ambitious agent as containing "a wealth of old plaster board". The kitchen was small, and the bathroom was large: the sitting-room and the bedroom were the two halves of what had once been a pretentious drawing-room. The ceilings were now unnaturally high in proportion to the floor area, but such had been the original amplitude that both rooms were still sizeable apartments. The floors were firm and the doors were solid, unlike those modern, smooth, hollow deceptions, which look so well, are so easy to clean, and so simple to smash. The sash windows were inclined to stick, but they were large, and at the back they looked down on a small garden, nicely kept by Miss Madrigal, who lived in the ground floor flat, and lived up to her name, being a great one for singing, not, it is true, the compositions of Morley or Byrd, but infallibly the music of an earlier age than this. Many a time, drowsing by the fire of an evening, Tito Adriano had heard Miss Madrigal's voice percolating through the floor boards. Sometimes it would be "Pale hands I loved beside the Shalimar": sometimes, with deeper abandon,

> Dearest, the dawn is breaking,
> Waneth the trembling moon—
> Hark, how the wind ariseth!
> Day will be here so soon.

Dangerous words which faded in and out in a mysterious manner as Miss Madrigal wandered about her domain from bedroom to bathroom, from sitting-room to kitchen. And then Tito Adriano would fall to wondering what Miss Madrigal was really like, for in a year's residence they had never yet passed each other in the hall and all he knew of her was a fore-shortened view of a generous behind, which he sometimes saw from the window, bending over the garden beds.

The other people in the house he occasionally passed on the stairs—Miss Prendergast from the second floor, Mr and Mrs Spinage from the third, and a sportive young couple from the top of the house called Swine and Minx (or so it appeared). It was an amiable household. No one ever bothered anyone else. Indeed, Amelia Gardens made a pleasant dwelling, though Fashion had deserted them and had shown no sign of repenting. Artistic nobs have rediscovered Canonbury and Islington, but Amelia Gardens are much too far away from anywhere, except Winston Manor.

The flat was convenient for Tito Adriano—just round the corner from Merton Road, and if ever he had found time to furnish it properly it would have been comfortable.

'God!' said Harriet throwing herself down on a cushion-covered divan. 'You do live in a pickle.'

'I have no one to look after me,' said Tito from the bedroom.

'You don't think I'm going to look after you, I hope.'

'Yes,' said Tito, walking briskly through the room, 'I do think that. You look after me, and I'll do the cooking.'

'What's on tonight?' called Harriet.

'Avocado soup,' said Tito from the kitchen.

'Gracious!'

'Cold pheasant.'

'That's too easy.'

'And fruta.'

'Fruta! That means all you're doing is avocado soup.'

'That's all there's time to do. It won't be two minutes.'

Standing in the doorway, Tito looked across the room at Harriet, lying sprawled on the divan, her black hair spread behind her like a mantilla, the red stones at her ears. She was half Spanish, and she looked it. Not precisely Carmen, Tito used to think, but certainly like one of her supporting friends from the factory.

'I hate Alan,' said Harriet calmly. 'And I hate Laura. But I hate Alan most. He's made a fool of me. I won't take the spurned wife from him or anyone else.'

'Do you want him?'

'No, of course I don't.'

'Then—'

'For God's sake don't be logical, Tito. That's no help at all. You know perfectly well why I've got to hang on to him.'

'A moment,' said Tito. 'The soup.'

'And the fool hasn't made a will,' Harriet called after him. 'He isn't even insured.'

'No?' said Tito. But he was paying more attention to the soup than to Harriet. Cooking and talking don't go together. That's the way to leave the sugar out of the lemon pudding, or the flour out of the sponge cake. Tito had done both in his time.

Attention: he had sieved the avocado, he had heated the chicken stock, and added the lemon juice: and now they must be blended with the cream and the curry powder. You were supposed to add cayenne, but Tito thought that was too much of a peppering. And, oh Lord yes, the parsley.

'Are you listening?' called Harriet.

'Yes. Isn't insured against what?'

'Isn't insured against anything.'

'Oh . . . You can come now. It's ready.'

'Good.'

'Some people add an egg yoke,' said Tito, absorbed in his achievement. 'And vermouth.'

'*Vermouth!*' said Harriet, settling down at the kitchen table.

'True. I've never tried it, but it sounds a bit odd to me.'

'How long have we got?'

'Half an hour.'

'The soup's marvellous,' said Harriet.

A little later, as he set the pheasant on the table, Tito said 'Are you coming tonight?'

'Yes.'

'You were there last night. I thought—'

'I've got to drive Alan home. So I may as well see it.'

It was not the basis of an entertaining conversation. Partly, they were in a hurry. Partly, there was a constraint between them. Neither wanted to talk about what was in their minds. And neither could think of anything else to talk about. They were both relieved when Tito said, 'Come on: it's past seven.'

A few minutes later they were driving very fast up Merton Road towards Winston Manor.

'Are all those people coming to the show?' asked Harriet.

'I expect so,' said Tito, steering through the school gateway. 'There's nothing better to do round here.'

They left the car in the small car park and walked down the path towards the theatre. Tito was moving towards the front entrance, but Harriet turned aside. 'You go on in,' she said. 'I shan't be sitting with you anyway.'

'O.K.,' said Tito amiably. Most amenable of men, sitting alone tonight, as it happened, was precisely what he preferred.

Harriet watched him enter the theatre. Then she turned back towards the house. There was a light in the room over the porch, which must mean that Priscilla was still working. She would pay her a visit, thought Harriet, entering the hall and stepping softly upstairs.

The landing was illuminated by a light which fell from the office, for the door was open, but, contrary to expectation, Miss Pringle was not within. The typewriter was set up for some manoeuvre, and a pile of forms lay on one side of the desk. On the other side was Priscilla's bag. It was half open, and so was one of the desk drawers, displaying, for the hand of any passing thief, stamps, insurance cards, keys, and other official treasures. Obviously Priscilla had been in the middle of something, but she was not there now. It reminded Harriet of the mystery of the *Marie Celeste*. Suppose Priscilla had disappeared altogether!

Returning to the doorway, she became aware of voices across the landing. Derek Wynter was talking to someone in the bursary. That would account for Priscilla. It was not very discreet, thought Harriet—not referring to the proprieties but only to the open drawer and the unguarded bag.

Harriet, incurably curious, found open drawers, open letters, and open bags irresistible. Very quietly she returned to the desk, and inspected the drawer. Then, after standing quite still for a precautionary two seconds, she opened the bag a little wider and peered inside that. Besides a purse and the familiar jumble of women there was something which gleamed. A brooch. Was it garnets? Harriet adored garnets. She slipped her hand into the bag and took the brooch out. But no, they were not garnets. Only brilliants. Harriet had an eye for these matters. But it was a pretty design. For a moment she held it against her dress and admired the picture in the office looking-glass. A business calendar behind one ear, a time-table behind the other, and, in between, Harriet. It was charming. A little reluctantly she dropped the brooch back into the hand-bag.

Then she went softly downstairs, and out into the garden. There was no one about. The show would be beginning in half a minute.

She walked down the path to the theatre.

x

Down at the wardrobe Mrs Goode looked at her watch and decided to pack it in. As Pomeroy had predicted, she had every intention of going to the show. Mrs Candour had been successfully taken in all round. And she had collected the tights and cod-pieces for the first year Shakespeare scenes. As she did so she had remembered with amusement last year's Malvolio. Poor boy, he'd only worn the tights. Never in the history of Shakespearean comedy had any scene gone so well. There seemed to be a laugh in every line and certain famous phrases had mysteriously acquired an additional significance. It had only been a fifteen minute scene, and luckily it had only been a school show in the small studio. But the few who saw it were never quite the same people again. It was the sort of joke that those old *commedia* actors might have played on purpose. But poor Desmond had not meant to be funny—at least, not in that way. Mrs Goode had felt sorry for Desmond—though truly, in some respects, the episode had enhanced his reputation.

Mrs Goode looked at her watch. Certainly it was time to stop. She put on her hat and coat, and felt for the key in her bag. She was always careful about locking up. Nobody else had the key to the wardrobe except Miss Pringle. And Miss Pringle, in Mrs Goode's opinion, was as reliable a woman as you could find this side of the Humber. Then she set off down the corridor to the canteen. As she went she could see the dressing-room doors ahead of her on the left curve. The first three were shut. The fourth made a rectangle of bright light in the green wall. That was dear little Laura's room : if she were there—

Laura was there. She was standing closely wrapped in Alan Bastable's arms.

Neither of them saw Mrs Goode pass by.

XI

There was quite a rattle of people walking down Merton Road. Mrs Pheasant and her daughter, Ruby, from No. 14, were going to the play, and so was Miss Mannering from Howarth Gardens

44

round the corner. Fifty years ago Miss Mannering had been Maudie Mannering—"One of the Boys" to audiences on Edwardian summer piers, who liked to see a fine girl bursting out of a morning suit with a top hat over one eye, twirling a malacca cane, and singing, *quasi parlando*, in a fruity baritone,

> It's ever so
> Jolly at
> Epsom . . .

In a slightly grosser mood it had also been Maudie Mannering who had made such a hit with

> Oh what an exposure
> In the Royal Enclosure
> When I put my shirt on
> A nice little filly

Miss Mannering was a little too inclined to sing that song still at the slightest sign of weakness among friends.

So, there they were, Mrs Pheasant and Ruby and Miss Mannering, walking together, and, overtaking them, some six characters who had got off the seven-ten bus at the Green Dragon stop—two men and a girl who had come to see Laura, a morose ex-actor who was covering the show for *The Stage*, and a handsome young man carrying a small suitcase who was walking with a younger, pretty young man, who had got into conversation with him on the bus on the important matter of just precisely where the Winston School was in relation to the Green Dragon.

'It's nice really,' Mrs Pheasant was saying, 'having the school so near. And it's a change from the old telly.'

'They can always count on me,' said Miss Mannering in a voice which still held baritone quality. 'I'm too old to play myself but I'm still game for a show. Always the old trouper.'

'That's just like you, Miss Mannering,' said Ruby.

And overlaying this, as Laura's friends passed by with quicker steps—

'Laura says we'll understand it when we see it.'

'I don't see how the masks help.'

'The girls don't wear them.'

'Don't they?'

'And not all the men.'

'It sounds a bit funny to me.'

'Silly! That's just what it's meant to be—funny.'

And then the two young men caught up.

'I'm coming because I want to see what it's like,' said the younger one eagerly. 'I've got an audition here soon—at least, I hope I have.'

'You might as well spin a coin,' said the other. 'I know. I've done it.'

'Have you? Are you a student here?'

'Not here—no—I'm at Renton's.'

'What's that like? . . .'

'One of these days,' said Miss Mannering, 'I shall sing them a song.'

'They'd be ever so pleased,' said Mrs Pheasant. 'You ought really to be on the telly, dear, and that's a fact.'

Miss Mannering twirled her umbrella in the air. Suddenly, and greatly to the consternation of Major Parkin, who had turned into the school drive just ahead of them, she announced to the darkling trees,

> 'I'm Johnny from Ascot
> The debutante's mascot—'

'I wish I'd heard you in the old days, Miss Mannering,' said Ruby. 'You must have been wonderful.'

'The audiences loved it, dear. And they'd love it again if they ever had the chance to hear the old songs sung in the right way.'

By the time they reached the foyer there was quite a

crowd: students, friends and relations of students, local supporters—like Mrs Pheasant, and Mr Monckton and Mrs Torriano, both of whom lived in Winston Crescent and were great supporters of the drama—a few adventurers from afar like Davie, one or two reporters, and even a couple of theatrical agents. Few knew what they were in for, but they were all prepared to be amused. The conversation, as Davie immediately noticed, had the right kind of anticipatory buzz about it.

Standing near the door, he was amusing himself watching faces. A jaunty young man, a show-off, an aged turkey cock: Harlequin, the Captain, Pantaloon—they're all here, thought Davie. The stage is only us.

Two gossiping old ladies. Two pretty girls. Two pretty young men. And Tito Adriano stepping up to speak to one of them.

'So you've come to see how it ought to be done, have you? Or do you think you can do it better anyhow?'

'I'll tell you when I've seen it, Tito. See you on Thursday?'

'Yes. Now watch this seriously. Criticize properly. They're quite good, this lot—especially *Il Dottore*.'

A bell pierced the chatter. Conversations changed course.

'Come along, Ruby,' said Mrs Pheasant. 'Have you got a programme?'

'Hurry up,' said Tito to the young man from the rival establishment, 'you mustn't be late.'

'I've just got to park my case.'

The second bell rang. Everyone started to move into the theatre. Davie's seat was in the second row, conveniently on the outside. There was just a minute to study the programme. There were two girls in the first piece—Flaminia and Isabella: and three in the second—Pantaloon's wife and his two daughters. Isabella and one of the daughters were played by Laura Darnton. Laura: that was the girl Martin Searle

47

had mentioned so gloomily—and doubtless the girl he had seen in the canteen with Alan Bastable. Vaguely Davie wondered if she were Mrs Goode's grand-daughter. Laura Darnton. It was a good programme name.

Then the house lights dimmed down to darkness and new lights rose on the stage. It is the modern version of the curtain—a new means to an old magic.

The play had begun.

<h1 style="text-align:center">XII</h1>

The Winston School Theatre was round, and the stage was potentially round, too. But it could be adjusted to any shape, and tonight that shape was only semi-circular, which meant that there were wings and side entrances up stage.

The play was, indeed, a familiar sort of story—not merely to a student of the *commedia dell'arte* but also to anyone knowing anything about eighteenth century comedy or those buffo operas which repeat each other so faithfully that one might almost suppose the form to be a necessary condition of composition. Pantaloon has a daughter, Flaminia. Flaminia has a suitor, Orazio. Orazio has a servant, Fabrizio, who turns out to be not a man but the fair Isabella in disguise. Isabella has run away from her father, the Doctor, to avoid the attentions of Flavio. Flavio, attended by his servant Arlecchino, pursues her. Captain Spavento (the boastful soldier) and his servant, Pedrolino, provide some cross purposes. And, in the end, Flavio wins over Isabella, and Orazio is rewarded with Flaminia. Everyone knows the plot, and fifty others of the same family. They range from Shakespeare and Molière to *The Barber of Seville* and *Don Pasquale*. It is not the story but the presentation that matters.

The actors of the old comedy worked not from a text but from a scenario. They depended on imagination, and wit, an ability to work together, each supporting the other, the business dovetailed. Select speeches—tags and soliloquies—might be memorized, but the play was not so much rehearsed as performed in an inevitable manner.

This swift accomplishment is not an art easily learned, and doubtless the young people on the stage of the Winston School were a dim reflection of the Italian comedians. Their performance was not more than a school exercise. But, because the actors went so bravely about it, they were good enough to delight Dr R. V. Davie. Too soon for him the stage lights faded, and the other lights rose slowly in the house.

That invisible curtain had come down again.

People began to get up for the interval. Glancing behind him as he rose, Davie noticed that Tito Adriano was just leaving the gangway seat of the back row—the seat Davie had briefly occupied earlier in the evening. It was the obvious place for a producer to sit. It gave him a chance to slip out at any time. And doubtless he *would* slip out later on, in order to be waiting in the wings for the invisible curtain call. The lady, Harriet, was not sitting with him. At the other end of the same row, equally convenient for an exit door, Davie spotted Martin Searle, the complete gentleman's understudy.

In the foyer he ran straight into Edward Pomeroy.

'How do you like it?' Pomeroy asked eagerly.

'Very, very much. Never again, I suppose, will actors command the same flow of improvised speech as the old players did. That was bred in the tongue, and in any case, so often repeated that it was in a sense memorized. It was improvised, but it was not new: the matter was eternally familiar. Your people just haven't got that experience—but within their competence they've made a glorious job of it. And how I adore those masks! You'd think they'd hamper the actor—'

'But they don't. They inspire him with their own naughtiness.'

'Exactly. It's a great and marvellous mystery.'

'Is your seat all right?'

'Fine.'

'I watch from a little private box at the back—but it's not comfortable enough for visitors. Shall I see you at the end? Would you like to go round afterwards and see the actors? I'm sure they'd be delighted.'

Most people eagerly accept an opportunity to "go behind". In a real professional theatre it is at once a privilege and an enchantment. The little hall by the door-keeper's office, the board with calls and messages, and in one corner that unexpected notice about the Actors' Church Union: the glimpse of the stage, lit by a working light, the back sides of the scenery—canvas and struts and three-ply—all flat and totally unconvincing. The stone stairs, the corridors, the doors with actors' names on them, and finally the little dedicated room itself, breathing artistic mystery. Paints, dresses, flowers, telegrams stuck in the looking-glass: the theatrical endearments. To most people it is "as good as a play", but to Davie it was an embarrassment. Actors were such strange people. If you called on an artist, or a writer, or a composer, you were not immediately expected to discuss their latest work. Indeed, many artists and writers are nervously unable to talk about their work at all. But an actor expects no other subject to be discussed in the dressing-room: and by discussion he means commendation. Davie liked the mysteries behind the scenes as much as anyone. But he resented the obligations, and since he was unwilling to offend, he paid no visits on actors. Besides, he liked to be home by a reasonable hour.

So, 'That's very kind of you,' he said, 'but I don't think I ought to linger. It will be late and I've some way to go. Perhaps I'll see you going out. But if I don't—thank you now for a really splendid evening.'

'Not a bit. I'm delighted you came. Forgive me now—I must have a word with that chap from *The Stage*.'

Davie stayed where he was, and listened to the babble of conversation going on around him.

'I can't stay for the second half,' Tito Adriano's young man was saying to his companion. 'I've got to see my mother in darkest Hertfordshire. See you some time.'

Then an elderly party on his other side: 'It's very amusing, *very* amusing, but it wouldn't have done for me, dear. You can't use a monocle in a mask and you can't wink. Of course I always had to wink. "It's ever so—jolly at—Epsom". *Wink*.' And here Miss Mannering winked boldly, once again to the confusion of Major Parkin, who was standing nearby and instantly assumed the familiarity to be personal. 'It would have spoilt it all without the wink,' said Miss Mannering. 'But they've got the audience laughing and that's the great thing.'

"It's ever so—jolly—at Epsom." That struck a chord somewhere in Davie's memory. Now who—but that was when the bell began to ring and diverted everyone's thoughts from whatever it was they were thinking or saying. Most people turned automatically towards the theatre. A few men, with a great air of concentration, scuttled off down the passage. Davie did not hurry. He was on the outside of a row.

Three minutes later everyone was in their places. The house lights dimmed to darkness and up came those other lights on the stage. The second half was away.

XIII

Up at the house, alone, and not in the least afraid of being alone, Miss Pringle finished her last form with a flourish—and then rested for a moment, like a solo pianist accepting the applause of a great audience. And, indeed, she did feel as though she were receiving the applause of a hundred happy recipients of her good words. She was well pleased. She had set herself a big task and she had accomplished it—in spite of interruptions. Poor Derek Wynter, thought Miss Pringle with a smile: he wasn't very good at his own sums.

Miss Pringle looked at her watch. It was fifteen minutes past nine. She got up and went to the uncurtained window. Outside everything was very still. Beyond the garden wall she could see the manifold lights of London. But the window was shut, and there was no sound of traffic. The play was not due to finish till twenty-five past. Ten minutes to go. Miss Pringle decided it was not really worth popping in for the end. She had seen the show before. What she wanted now was a cup of coffee, and the canteen was still open. So she put on her coat, tied a scarf round her head, locked the office door, crossed the landing and descended the beautiful old stairs. As she did so she thought how ugly the hygienic staircase was at Crofton Mansions where she maintained her own less ample establishment. She hated those shining composition treads and the dark green walls, and the horrid brown paint of the banisters. Spending her days in the faded elegance of Winston Manor had spoiled Miss Pringle for the pleasures of modern convenience.

Even outside the house it was quiet. If you listened you might hear a gentle purr of motor-cars and buses—but if you didn't listen, thought Miss Pringle, if you thought about the grass and the trees, it was just like being in the country. The dark clouds of the early evening had disappeared. Outside in the street, in the lamplight, one might not notice the moon: but here, in the garden, there truly was genuine moonlight, making shadows of the trees on the lawn.

Miss Pringle walked down the path and entered the theatre by the side door. This was that circular corridor round the back of the theatre where Mr Pomeroy had brought Davie that afternoon. Passing the wardrobe on the left, the passage curved between the dressing-rooms and the back of the stage. It was an ingenious arrangement—four steps across the passage and the actor was in the wings. And indeed, just ahead of her, an actor was crossing the corridor at that moment. It was Peter Niccolini, only one generation removed from Italy, but cockney born and cockney spoken. He was the man who played the Doctor. Unlike most of the staff, Miss Pringle rather liked Peter. She waved a friendly hand towards him, and he waved pompously back at her—pompously because that self-satisfied nose made everything pompous. The next moment he had disappeared through the O.P. pass door.

From the auditorium came a gust of laughter.

'Good,' said Miss Pringle, stepping daintily on towards the canteen. 'It's going well.' Then she pushed open the door with the circular window and said, 'Maureen—for pity's sake give me a cup of coffee—and if you've got an iced bun—'

'There's just one left, Miss Pringle.'

'There is! Bless you! I'm starving.'

XIV

The second half was more like a vaudeville entertainment—every man in his humour. They were all on the stage except Pantaloon: the Doctor boring away—"A ship upon the high seas cannot be said to be in port"—while Clown, mistaking him for a statue, made play with a feather duster and was not particular about where he applied it.

Pantaloon only came on towards the end. It appeared that he was concerned with business and wanted to be left alone. But everyone would talk to him—his wife, his daughters, the Captain, the Doctor, Harlequin. Pantaloon would oblige none of them: he wouldn't even answer: he was busy doing his accounts. Finally, to escape their attentions, he flounced off the stage, pursued by the whole rout. (And, how splendid! thought Davie. The *pursuit*, the great climax of the Keystone Comedies: the influence of the *commedia* runs everywhere.) Then back across the stage streamed the baffled pursuers, and when they had safely disappeared, out came the cunning old gentleman from behind a pillar. Now at last he could get on with his work. He returned to his chair and opened his book. But then, sneakingly, in came the Captain. Suddenly he put a noose round the old man's neck and attempted to strangle him. Pantaloon sat on, calmly reading. Amazed, the Captain produced a great mallet and hit him on the head. Pantaloon raised a hand and stroked his head as though annoyed by a fly, but on his finger a ruby ring sparkling in the light. Then the Captain attacked him with a vast dagger. He could not push it in. Apparently the old fool had the hide of a rhinoceros. The Captain gave up. But then in came Pantaloon's wife and smacked him lightly with her fan, and Pantaloon collapsed into a wheelbarrow. Everyone rushed on to look, Clown wheeled him off, stage right, and down came the invisible curtain. . . .

When the lights went up again the stage was empty—and, one by one, from the centre opening, beginning with Clown, the actors came forward to make their bow. One by one, till there were two lines on either side of the stage. Then they all looked back as though expecting somebody else. Nobody came. Then Columbine (one of Pantaloon's daughters) looked to the left instead, and held out a hand, and in came Tito Adriano and took his place in the centre of the line. Everybody bowed, and then Adriano turned round and bowed to the cast—displaying as he did so a patch of white on his left shoulder—like something rubbed off a white-washed wall. Clown instantly nipped forward and dusted him with his feather brush. It was a nice touch. The audience laughed and renewed their applause. Was this rehearsed, Davie wondered, or was it "improvisation"? Whatever it was, it was good. Then the lights went down and up, down and up, and down. And then they stayed down. And the house lights went up, and the show was over, and everyone made for the exits.

Davie was very well placed, and since he had nobody else to consider, he was in fact the first person on the garden path. Or almost the first. There was a car moving out of the small car park near the house. He watched the headlights stabbing the bushes beside the drive, and leaving sudden darkness behind as the car passed through the gates. There was also a man who was a bit ahead of him, and who seemed to be part of the establishment, for he had branched off along a side path that led to the house. There was a light over the door and for a moment, as he mounted the steps, his face was illuminated. It was the man Davie had seen in the bursar's office. Presumably he was the bursar.

I didn't notice him in the theatre, thought Davie, as he walked on down the drive.

Curtain calls: this business with the lights was new to Davie. If you hadn't got a curtain it was the only thing to do: and certainly it was effective. As he left the moonlit garden and stepped into the lamplight Davie found himself remembering how totally the critics had disapproved of curtain calls when that fashion first invaded the nineteenth century. Garrick had never taken curtain calls, nor had Mrs Siddons. And truly it is an absurdity—all those Macbeths and Othellos and Romeos ridiculously staggering to their feet, restored to life by the elixir of applause. Not that he didn't enjoy the curtain calls. He did. They had become part of the show. But you could bet your life they would have puzzled the actors of the old *commedia*. So Davie was thinking as he made his way down Merton Road. But as soon as he had crossed the main road and stationed himself by the bus stop, there were other things to consider—faces to watch and scraps of talk to overhear, and when the bus came up a few moments later he had forgotten about curtain calls and was speculating on the relationship between a prim young man and a miraculously ugly young woman. They had been holding hands but had had nothing to say to each other. For both their sakes he hoped it was the end of the evening's entertainment: but they both got on the bus, and went inside. Davie never did that if he could help it. Dangerously swaying as the bus went round the corner, he hauled himself up the steep stairs and was pleased to find the back seat empty.

The front seat or the back seat, those were the places to ride on top of a bus. It was odd to think that in the twenties, less than fifty years ago, the top deck had been open to the sky. It had been fun in the sunshine, hell in the rain. On the back of the seats there had been little canvas aprons which could be drawn over the knees. Much use that had been. And the seats, open to the weather, had been plain wood and damned hard.

And then Davie's thoughts went further backwards still. It wasn't only the unroofed bus that he remembered. Somewhere about 1904 he could distinctly see himself riding on the top of a bus in the sunshine and looking down on the broad backs of horses.

Horses! Another world! He had ridden in a ponycart, a dogcart (that smart turn out with the big wheels), a brake, a hansom, a hackney cab, a victoria, a landau, a brougham, and in a country railway station bus, a vehicle not far removed from the stage coach. They were all gone now. That was natural. What was surprising was that he, Dr Davie, addict of the aeroplane, should remember them.

And then, suddenly, the bus came to a stop, and, looking down, he found himself regarding the lights of Oxford Street. Dreaming about horses, those dream-like creatures, he had forgotten about machines. He only just managed to get off the bus in time.

'Good night,' said Davie.

'Good night, guv',' said the bus conductor. 'Mind how you go.'

'Guv': he always enjoyed being called that.

It was a pleasant quiet walk back to the Chesterfield through side streets, quite empty at this time of night. It's ever so—jolly at—Epsom, hummed Davie, as he stepped along the pavement. De-diddle-de-diddle-de-dum. He couldn't remember the words—but, of course, yes, it was Maudie Mannering who had sung them. He'd heard her do it on a pier somewhere, and at the Holborn Empire. She never stopped singing it. He could still recall that chesty voice. He could even remember the wink. De-diddle-de-diddle-de-dum . . . He wished he could remember the words. But they were gone, gone with the halls and the horses.

X V

It was not particularly late when he entered the Chesterfield—but he decided to go up to his room. He was tired, and he did not even try to read in bed. He snipped out the light and lay on his back thinking about the old Italian actors and their enormous influence upon every form of comedy. Harlequin and Pantaloon and the Inn-keeper and the Doctor and the Captain and Clown: they were all manifestations of basic joys, jokes which have ruled the world. There had been an excellent Doctor that night. And a very good Pantaloon—but—that's odd, thought Davie, suddenly opening his eyes and staring at the window curtains: Pantaloon had not taken his curtain call. That was why everyone had looked to the centre just before Tito Adriano came on from the left. They were expecting Pantaloon. Why hadn't he come on? It is not good professional behaviour to throw temperaments—but the students of the Winston School were not fully fledged: perhaps Alan Bastable had been behaving like a *prima donna*: he was obviously an intemperate person.

Or perhaps, thought Davie, rolling over on his side . . . But he went no further with that speculation. Suddenly and deliciously he became uninterested in the answer.

De-diddle-de-diddle-de-dum, said Dr Davie, and fell into a gentle sleep.

PART TWO

THE TRAGEDY

'HULLO, DAVIE! WE haven't met since the Pope demoted the patron saint of your college. I was sorry about that.'

It was half past ten, and George Canteloupe had just discovered Davie in the morning-room.

'What about your own saint?' Davie answered. 'George has had it, too. The authors of the *Acta Sanctorum* seem to have been singularly at fault. If they have been so grossly misinformed about the merits and even the existence of Nicholas, Christopher, George, Barbara, and Catherine, how are we to know if they're right about anyone else?'

'Precisely.'

'Fortunately our college has never been dependent upon Nicholas alone. We are also under the protection of St Athanasius and the Magnificent Virgin Edwina. I expect I've told you about her.'

'Remind me.'

'She took refuge in our monastery, miraculously convinced everyone that she possessed the suitable attributes of a male, and so escaped the vile pursuit of one Egglewulf, a pagan lord of the East Anglian marshes.'

'Well—that's something,' said Canteloupe gravely. 'I'm glad you're not left wholly unprotected in this dangerous world. But surely this demotion is easier said than accomplished. They may take away Nicholas's halo, but they can't expect you to start talking about Nicholas College.'

'We certainly will not.'

'And what,' said Canteloupe warmly, for it was a point which touched him nearly, 'what about—

"Cry God for Harry, England, and George!"

Dammit! It doesn't scan. It won't do at all.' Then, suddenly lowering his vast body into a deep armchair, he said, 'How nice to see you, R.V. How long are you down for?'

'Two or three nights. Last night I went to a *commedia dell'arte* show at a drama school. And tonight—'

'You're going to the opera.'

'Yes—*Ariadne on Naxos* at the Coliseum.'

'Which is also *commedia dell'arte*, if I remember rightly.'

'Yes, it is—in part.'

But there their conversation was interrupted. The door opened, and Craddock, the Chesterfield's aged hall porter, advanced into the room.

'There's a call for you, Dr Davie,' he said. 'In box three.'

'Oh bother! Do you know who it is?' Davie had a particular distaste for mystery voices.

'It was a lady, sir, a Miss Pringle, I think.'

'Pringle?' said Davie considerably alarmed. '*Pringle?* I don't know anyone called Pringle.'

'The lady said it was important,' said Craddock.

'Drat it,' said Davie. 'But I—'

'Go on,' said George Canteloupe. 'Be a man.'

And so Davie made his reluctant way to box three, gingerly lifted the receiver, and said in a very quiet voice, as though he hoped that might lend him some special protection, 'This is R. V. Davie speaking.'

'I'm so glad to have found you, Dr Davie,' said an eager voice in his ear. 'I'm Miss Pringle. We met at the Winston School yesterday, I'm Mr Pomeroy's secretary.'

'Ah,' said Davie, suddenly relieved of a desperate anxiety. 'Yes—of course. What can I do for you, Miss Pringle?'

'I'm afraid I can't explain it properly on the telephone, Dr Davie, but there's been a terrible tragedy at the school, and it's important that we should locate everyone who was at the theatre

62

last night. It isn't easy to trace them all, and some of them aren't on the telephone—but I'm so glad I've managed to find you. Mr Pomeroy would be most grateful if you could spare the time to come out—'

'What—now?'

'Yes, please, if you possibly can. It's very important. You see, one of our actors has been killed, and the police have to take depositions.'

'The police, eh?'

'Yes—you see . . .' Somewhere in North London Miss Pringle took a deep breath. 'You see—it wasn't an accident, Dr Davie.'

For three seconds neither of them spoke. Then, 'Do you mean it was one of your actors last night?' Davie asked quietly.

'Yes—Alan Bastable—the boy who played Pantaloon.'

'I know who you mean . . . You said "boy": how old was he?'

'Twenty-six: he was one of the older ones. Will you be able to come up, Dr Davie?'

'Yes, certainly,' said Davie. 'I'll come at once.'

II

Mr Pomeroy was still wearing the fawn suit. And the probability was that he had never taken it off. He was looking tired out and ten years older.

'Thank you for coming so promptly,' he said. 'A fair number of the audience was from the school—which was easy: and some were locals, and they could be found. But the few who came from a distance have to be pursued. We were fortunate to find you so soon. It's a routine matter. There has been a death . . .' Mr Pomeroy paused as though he were considering the adequacy of the last word. Then he began again. 'There has been a murder. It was committed almost in sight of a large number of people. Also some of the visitors may not have been where they were supposed to be—may have changed seats, or have left early. The police just want to ask each member of the audience where they were sitting, and if they noticed anything unusual at the end of the play.'

'Somebody will be sure to see something significant in the Captain's repeated attempts to assassinate Pantaloon.'

'Yes,' said Mr Pomeroy, and said no more.

'You'd like me to go down to the theatre and make my statement.'

'Yes, please.'

Davie hesitated. 'Aren't you going to tell me what happened?'

'We don't know.'

'No, of course you don't. I only meant—am I entitled to ask what was discovered, and when, and where?'

'You will understand, Dr Davie,' said Mr Pomeroy, 'that if I were to give an account to each person of what apparently happened, it would take a long time. And it might put ideas into people's heads which would not naturally have been there at all. They would begin remembering things they never saw. The police don't want me to say too much about it.'

Davie nodded. 'Yes, yes. You are entirely right.'

'On the other hand, a good number of people do know the facts, and one can't really keep them a secret. Alan Bastable was bowled off the stage in a wheelbarrow. The chap who played Clown can testify that he was alive then. He got out of the wheelbarrow as soon as they were off. Then the lights went down. The cast left the stage and re-entered in turn for their calls. But Bastable did not come on.'

'I noticed that.'

'Coming off stage after a show the actors are full of their own excitements. They did not immediately start asking where he was. Tito Adriano was walking round the dressing-rooms, and he, of course, did ask for him. And so did Harriet—that's his wife. She'd been at the show and came round to pick him up. Michael Teed, who shared a room with him, hadn't seen

64

him. It was assumed, I expect, that he was having one of his tantrums. Anyhow, nobody made a fuss about looking for him. And then, some time later, when nearly everyone had gone, one of the stage hands found him hidden under some material behind a curtain in the wings, close by the place where he would have been standing, waiting to go on. He had been stabbed in the back.

'Nobody knows a thing about what happened. All we know is what was discovered half an hour afterwards.'

'I see. No one in the audience could possibly have witnessed what occurred. In addition to which the lights were going down and up, and people were fishing for coats and umbrellas. And yet somebody somewhere may have seen something which has some bearing on the problem.'

'That is precisely it.'

'Thank you for telling me,' said Davie, rising. 'I'll go down to the theatre.'

'The front entrance,' said Pomeroy. 'You'll find an officer there to direct you.'

III

Davie's interview with the police lasted four minutes. They took his address. They made a note of his seat on the theatre plan. They asked him if he had seen anything strange at the end of the play. Only, he said, that everyone had looked towards the centre opening as though expecting someone to come on. The police officer nodded his head and made a brief note. Obviously he already knew that, probably from the actors.

Davie had nothing else to tell him. And so he walked through the foyer, raised a valedictory hand to the policeman on duty, and passed through the swing doors on to the garden path. And there he was, all ready to set off back to the club—except that he had no umbrella. He remembered then that he had left it in Mr Pomeroy's office, and so he walked up the path to the house, and mounted the stately stairs, even in those dramatic circumstances giving a thought, as he went, to the late Sir William Button.

The door of Miss Pringle's office stood open, and Miss Pringle was waiting for him in the doorway.

'I saw you through the window,' she said. 'Mr Pomeroy had to go out. So he brought your umbrella in here.'

'Thank you very much,' said Davie. 'One loses an appalling number of umbrellas.'

'You've had your interview?'

'Yes.'

'Isn't this a terrible thing?' said Miss Pringle. It was obvious that she wanted to talk. 'Do you know, I must have walked past the very place only five minutes before it happened. You see, I'd been working late and I went down to the theatre to get a cup of coffee in the canteen. I went in by the side door and walked down the corridor that runs behind the stage.'

'I know. I saw it yesterday. And you were there—when?'

'Five minutes before the end of the show. I know because the canteen clock said twenty-two minutes past, and that's always kept fast. The show ended at twenty-five past—and that was when it happened. Alan was on stage till the end of the piece—and then when it came to the curtain call he was dead. One can hardly believe it.'

'And you didn't see anything or anybody?'

'No one at all—except Peter. He was just crossing the corridor.'

'Peter?'

'Peter Niccolini—he's the boy who plays the Doctor.'

'Did he see nobody?'

'No one. I asked him myself.'

'If neither of you saw anyone, there was no one to see,' said Davie. 'But that was about four minutes before Pantaloon came off stage. Much can happen in four minutes.'

'Yes.' From the alert expression on Miss Pringle's face it was clear that she would gladly have continued the conversation. But Davie, thinking it wiser to go, said 'Goodbye, Miss Pringle: you know where to find me if I should be wanted again.' And so Miss Pringle had to say goodbye too. 'And thank you, Dr Davie, for coming. I'm afraid its taken up a lot of your day.'

Walking down the drive, Davie was thinking four minutes is a long time. The person only had to be in the right position to strike just before Bastable was due to take his call.

But a quarter of an hour later, comfortably settled on top of a homeward bus, he told himself that that couldn't be the answer, not the whole answer. Miss Pringle saw no one—but if she'd been only a little later she might have done. No one would take such a crazy risk. Unless—unless there was something natural, something acceptable, in that person being there: the stage-manager, for instance, or a stage hand.

Stopping and starting, the bus bowled on. Bells rang. But Dr Davie, usually a delighted observer of the London pageant, saw nothing, heard nothing. Lost in thought, he stared straight ahead of him at a woman's hat two seats further along the deck. It was blue, round, and whorled to a peak like some obscene meringue. For Davie it was as a crystal, as a bowl of water to a seer. In those azure involutions he reviewed the happenings of the previous day. Pomeroy, Mrs Goode, the rehearsal, Martin Searle, the show, the curtain call—and, just now, Miss Pringle's interesting evidence.

Once he snapped his finger and thumb together and said out loud, 'I wouldn't have thought that was possible: and yet, apparently it happened.' But there was no light of discovery in his eyes, no guilty desire to interfere. Dr Davie had not yet surrendered to an old temptation.

IV

That night Davie got to the Coliseum in good time, had an amiable word with the programme seller (an old friend from the days when Sadler's Wells was at Sadler's Wells) and made his way to his seat in the front row. In that great theatre the nearer the better in his opinion.

A great theatre, with what memories of sublime Variety! Lily Morris in the first half of the programme singing "Don't have any more, Mrs More": and, in the second half, the Diaghilev ballet—*Les Sylphides* and those thrilling savage dances from *Prince Igor*. Once, round about 1916, he had seen Mrs Langtry attempting a come-back in a one act play. Mrs Langtry! Truly, memory was the prize for making a high score.

Tonight he was looking forward to the performance very much. He liked *Ariadne,* and now it promised an additional interest. There are *commedia* characters in this work. It would be interesting to compare them with the characters he had seen on the previous night at the Winston School.

First, he studied the programme for a few seconds. Ariadne was new: so was Bacchus: but the rest of the singers he had heard several times in these parts. He could see them all in his head, and for a minute he reviewed their story.

Act One of *Ariadne* is set behind the scenes of a private theatre in the house of "the richest man in Vienna" on the night of a sumptuous entertainment. A crash decision has been made that the specially commissioned opera must in some manner be cut and performed coincidentally with the *commedia dell'arte* play which was to have followed it. This contrivance, the actors are informed, is absolutely necessary if the stage performance is to be finished in time for the fireworks at nine o'clock. The singers are distracted, the composer is in despair—but the *commedia* actors, used to this sort of thing, are confident they can carry it off. And in the second act they do so to perfection—weaving in and out of the opera with exquisite discretion—the lady, Zerbinetta, and her gentlemen admirers, Harlequin, Scaramuccio, Truffaldino, and Brighella.

In the second act, when they are "performing", these male characters are masked: but in the first act, when they are behind the scenes, before the opera within the opera begins, they are themselves. It was, Davie thought, a rare opportunity to see how complete a disguise a half-mask really was. Would one remember—except for particular slimness or fatness, except for quality of voice—who was playing what? He did not think he would.

But now tuning sounds in the orchestra recalled him from the island of Naxos. Pocketing his programme, Davie peeped over the rail to see how they were getting on down there: then he looked over his shoulder to see how the house was filling up: and then he looked up with customary pleasure to the two groups of golden lions, poised on the roofs of the highest boxes, either side of the proscenium. These splendid beasts would have leapt into the auditorium long ago had it not been for the powerful arms of the two gallant youths who hold them in leash.

Davie was greatly attached to these ferocious creatures, fixed in a posture, and restrained for ever from devouring Christians in the Coliseum arena below. But the poor things were deplorably dusty, and in their inaccessible position were likely to remain so. Someone, thought Davie, should go up in a balloon and attend to them.*

It was a welcome and plangent oboe which brought him back to the stalls—that clarion which suddenly arrests the diversity of noises in an orchestra pit. It is as good as a call boy. Everyone begins to settle down. It brought Davie to attention immediately. Only two minutes now and the house lights would go down, the door to the left of the orchestra would open, the conductor would make his way between the players, mount the rostrum, shake hands with the leader (a strange formality that: they have met before), bow to the audience, glance quickly and confidently at his players, and then raise his expressive hands.

It is a ceremony that never fails to stir the heart.

* *Publisher's note*: Someone has now done so, but not, alas, in a balloon.

V

Two hours and a bit later, standing in the gutter outside the
theatre, in imminent danger of being debreeched by the passing
traffic, an aged busker was giving a vigorous performance on two
spoons, to the accompaniment of a decrepit banjo played by
another aged busker. In memory of other days Davie dropped a
sixpence in the greasy cap lying on the pavement. Fifty years
ago buskers were common, they moved from queue to queue,
claiming territorial rights to particular pitches at particular times.
Now, with all seats bookable, the queues have vanished with the pit
and cheap prices—except cinema queues, and their hearts are not
in the same places. And so you don't see buskers much nowadays,
except sometimes outside a theatre after the show—like these two
old things tonight, hammering away hell for leather. They had
only about ten minutes to do it in. And so Davie dropped a sixpence as a passing tribute to another age, crossed the road, and
made his way zigzag through the horrid crowds of Leicester
Square, Coventry Street and Piccadilly Circus, eventually emerg-
ing unscathed on the sedate pavements of Piccadilly.

St James's Church, the Royal Academy, Fortnum and Mason,
the Burlington Arcade, Bond Street, the Ritz, and then the
greenest of all parks—in this age of destruction it must be one of
the least altered stretches in all London, apart from the loss of
the Berkeley Hotel.

Coming through the crowds Davie had had to concentrate on
navigation. Now, in these calmer reaches, he could return to the
evening's entertainment. And in particular to those actors in
masks. It had been as he had said to Pomeroy last evening,
'Pomeroy, thou art translated'. Except for one fat figure, you
could not remember who was playing what. In some extraordinary way the mask takes charge. He had seen several actors in
these parts—but when the masks were on they were all the same.
They became the mask.

Now in Verdi's *Masked Ball*, Davie told himself, the position is quite different. In the last act the whole company wears little black masks, just covering the eyes—and the action is ridiculous. Which is the King? Why, that one over there, of course. No one could doubt it for a moment. The point is that the people at the masked ball are not acting up to a mask with features: they are playing at being disguised, and not really wanting to be unrecognized. Those are not masks in the *commedia* tradition. It is merely high society indulging in a frolic.

But, said Davie, arguing with himself as he turned into Half Moon Street, suppose in some *commedia* play the actors were miming, not talking, and suppose there were not vast differences of figure among the actors, then one would never be certain which player was behind which mask. One might expect to know. One might think one knew. But one could be wrong.

One could be wrong, he repeated—and then, part way along Half Moon Street, he suddenly stood still and asked why he was kidding himself. He knew perfectly well why he had been so interested in the behaviour of the actors tonight. A thought had been stirring in his mind all the afternoon, a thought which had begun on the top of the bus on the way home from Winston School . . . Miss Pringle had said that she had seen Peter Niccolini in the corridor about five minutes before the end of the show. Davie thought that this was untrue. He was not questioning Miss Pringle's integrity. He was questioning her powers of observation. But if he were right, if Miss Pringle had been mistaken, what would it mean? And ought he to leave it alone, or ought he to uncover his mind to Mr Pomeroy?

In his perplexity he walked straight past a black and white cat without saying good night—which, for Davie, was an unprecedented discourtesy. As indeed the black and white cat seemed to think, for he skipped past him, tail in air, and stationed himself on a doorstep a little way ahead, as though to give the gentleman another chance. This time Davie stopped to stroke him. 'You are a very handsome cat,' he said. 'A very handsome cat indeed. Have a good time.'

When he moved on the cat bounded ahead and sat down on another doorstep, as though anxious to repeat such an agreeable encounter. But here unfortunately was Davie's turning. He could only wave a hand and echo the words of the bus conductor. 'Good night, Guv. Mind how you go.'

As soon as he turned the corner he was back with his problem. Certainly he would not confide his thoughts to the police without sure confirmation of the suspicion that was whispering to him at the back of his mind. But he could not get confirmation without asking certain questions, and he could only do that with the permission of Mr Pomeroy. Getting in touch again would be a little embarrassing. But he was sure that that was what he was going to do.

VI

And so it was that Davie made the journey to the Green Dragon for the third time in three days; and, when he had told Edward Pomeroy the strange thought that he had in his mind, Edward Pomeroy sent for Peter Niccolini and asked if he would help them.

'In newspaper language,' said Davie, 'the word "help" has a dreadful significance. The man who is "helping the police" is the chap who's being badgered into a confession. We really do want your assistance. A strange matter has come to my notice, and I think you are the only person who can help us to explain it.'

'I'll do what I can,' said Peter Niccolini. But not willingly, thought Davie: he's nervous.

'Miss Pringle has told me that you and she were both near the spot where Alan Bastable was killed, and only a few

72

minutes before it happened: but that neither of you saw anyone else. She said she asked you about it.'

'Yes, she did—but I didn't really know what she was talking about. She said, "Did you see anyone? It was so near the time," and I said no I hadn't, which was true. But I didn't really understand when she meant.'

'That is my point,' said Davie. 'You didn't know what, or when, she meant because you were on the stage, or briefly in the wings, and didn't have any chance to see anyone.'

'Yes,' said Peter Niccolini, and suddenly blushed a deep rose.

'Miss Pringle is under the impression that she saw you in the corridor five minutes before the end of the show.'

'I was on the stage.'

'That is what I supposed. Yet Miss Pringle saw someone dressed for the part of the Doctor, crossing the corridor to the O.P. door. Miss Pringle isn't blind. If it wasn't you, there must have been two Doctors in the theatre then.'

Peter Niccolini said nothing. 'We don't want to tell this story to the police, Peter,' said Pomeroy, 'unless we're sure it has some bearing on their problem. But if we can't explain it, then I suppose we'll have to tell them.'

'I'm sorry, I can't help you.'

'I think you can a little,' said Davie, 'if you don't mind answering a few questions.'

'O.K.'

'You would have been either on stage or in the wings on the prompt side?'

'Yes.'

'This character reached the stage by the O.P. door. Therefore he could have been in the wings on the other side of the stage but not visible to you.'

'Yes.'

'What other characters would have used the O.P. side?'

'None of them, at that time. They all run across the stage

to the prompt side, and it's from that side that they crowd on at the end.'

'Yes. I remember it was like that. So there wouldn't have been anyone on the O.P. side?'

'Not till Clown wheeled Pantaloon off in the barrow.'

'And then Clown was the first to go on for the call?'

'Yes.'

'That would have left Pantaloon alone on that side?'

'Yes.'

'Am I asking you the same sort of questions the police asked?'

'Not quite. They wanted to know who was where—but where in regard to Pantaloon. You are interested—'

'In the Doctor.'

'I was on stage or in the wings on the prompt side, except for that second or so when we all chased after Pantaloon to the O.P. side—'

'And then ran back again.'

'Yes.'

'That was all I wanted to know. Thank you very much for telling me.'

'Is that all?'

'Yes,' said Pomeroy. 'Thanks, Peter. Don't say anything to anyone about this. At the moment it's rather like a ghost story. Priscilla has seen someone who doesn't exist.'

'O.K., Edward.'

For a few seconds Davie and Pomeroy sat in silence. Both of them were listening to Peter Niccolini's steps as he went down the oak staircase.

Then, 'What do you make of that?' asked Pomeroy.

'I don't believe in phantoms,' said Davie. 'It seems clear that someone dressed as the Doctor entered the O.P. wings shortly before the end of the play.'

'Clown would have seen him.'

'If he were expecting Clown and the barrow, he could have hidden behind a curtain.'

'Alan would have known that he oughtn't to have been there.'

'Alan wouldn't have had much time to know anything. Besides, if the costume was convincing he would have accepted it, just for a fatal few seconds.'

'Anything else?'

'Yes. I didn't think our Doctor—'

'Peter?'

'Yes. I didn't think he was altogether happy. I agree that he can't have been in the corridor, and yet it seemed to me that he was not comfortable—as though somehow he was aware of the encounter although it hadn't been with him. Did that strike you?'

'No, it didn't. But perhaps I wasn't thinking along the same lines. Questions often embarrass people. If you ask the charlady if she's seen a dropped coin, she always thinks you're accusing her of stealing.'

'That's true. And if a policeman comes to the door with an innocent enquiry, one always feels guilty of some unknown crime before he's opened his mouth. There is one point: is Miss Pringle short sighted?'

'Yes, she is.'

'She doesn't wear glasses.'

'She does when she chooses.'

'But, the corridor being curved, she must have been fairly close to this person, or she wouldn't have seen him at all.'

'One could check that.'

'So—glasses or no glasses—I would have thought that Miss Pringle did see what she thought she saw.'

'Yes.'

'And that that person was not a member of the cast.'

'I suppose I ought to tell the police.'

'I suppose you should.'

'The inspector's coming to see me at two o'clock,' said Edward Pomeroy.

VII

Looking down at the paving stones, his hands together in that monkish manner he unconsciously adopted when occupied with distant speculations, Davie was making his way back along Merton Road. He walked straight through the hop-scotch chalk marks on the pavement, trod upon an exhortation to Tottenham Hotspurs, and stepped delicately over a rude word. But he saw none of these things. He was thinking of the Doctor of Bologna.

The traffic at the cross-roads brought him back to London. And there he was, outside the Green Dragon. He looked at his watch. It was half past twelve—too late to get back to the Chesterfield. He decided to get something in the pub. He did not feel like a dining-room lunch. But there would be something in the bar. Not, on any account, sandwiches—those disastrous devices for inducing a man to eat two days' supply of bread in about ten minutes flat. But there would be cold beef for a certainty, and celery, and cheese: that was all right: and a little glass-topped table to eat it at if you didn't want to perch on a stool at the bar. And to drink, perhaps a gin and tonic. It was a pity, but an Englishman's beer was sudden death, and cider instant sleep: it would have to be gin and tonic.

There were not many people in the bar. The Green Dragon was more of an evening place of resort. Davie gave his order and retired to a little table in a corner. And there, sipping his gin and tonic, he studied the sporting prints. How alike they all were, he was thinking. Always the same lean characters taking the fences, and the same fat characters not taking them, scrambling from hedges and ditches and ponds, while the hunt streaks down the hill towards the stream and the neatly drawn woods in the middle distance. The scene was as predictable as a carousal of cardinals in that other strange tradition of bright painting.

Presently they brought him the beef and the celery and the cheese: it was all excellent.

Peter Niccolini and Martin Searle did not see Davie when they came in. For several minutes they stood at the bar, heads together over two glasses of beer. They were deep in some serious conversation. Probably, Davie thought, Niccolini was already betraying the story of his recent interview. And then Niccolini turned his head, saw him, and blushed, as he had that morning, blushed the colour of a rose. Martin Searle followed his glance, and Davie raised a hand gravely in recognition.

Then the two young men turned away and spoke quickly together, and apparently came to a decision, for Martin Searle crossed the room to Davie's table and said, 'Can Peter and I talk to you about something, please? It's rather important.'

'Yes, of course you can,' said Davie. 'Have you something to drink?'

'Yes, thanks.'

Searle turned and beckoned to Niccolini. Still blushing deeply, Niccolini joined them.

'Sit down,' said Davie. 'What's the trouble?'

For a second Martin Searle and Peter Niccolini looked at one another, uncertain who would speak first. Then Martin said, 'Peter says you've spotted the two Doctors. Well, the second one was me. I'm sorry we've introduced a false scent—but of course we hadn't any idea what was going to happen.'

'It was the worst possible luck,' said Peter.

'Why did you do it?' Davie asked.

'Just to see if we could. I said the mask was a complete disguise, provided the voices weren't too different. You remember when the characters all chase after Pantaloon, stage right.'

'Yes.'

'Well, Peter slipped behind a curtain and I took his place when they all chased back again. After that the Doctor has very little to say apart from the general hubbub. I reckoned I could get away with it. And I did, as far as the stage was concerned. The trouble was that Priscilla saw me in the corridor, and happened to mention it to you. If you hadn't been so observant

77

you wouldn't have known that the Doctor couldn't have been there at that time. It was only a joke. But we didn't want to own up to it. And, as it was perfectly harmless, we didn't say anything to the police. But now you've found out about it we don't know what to do.'

Several seconds went by before Davie replied. Then he said, 'I'll tell you what I think, if you'll answer a few questions.'

'Certainly,' said Martin. 'O.K.,' said Peter.

'You went—where, after coming off stage?' Davie asked Peter.

'To my room. I share it with the chaps who play Harlequin and Clown. The idea was that I stayed there, so that nobody should see me. Then, when the company came off, it would only look as though I'd got first to the dressing-rooms. Martin had a little cubby-hole on the stage where he could get out of his things.'

'You came straight off stage as soon as you could?'

'As soon as Pantaloon was back on stage.'

'Was your room in sight of either of the stage doors?'

'Yes—the O.P. door.'

'Did you see anyone in the corridor?'

'Well—naturally, I wasn't looking. I wasn't there, so to speak. There could have been someone.'

'But you saw no one?'

'No one strange. I did see Tito. He came down the corridor and went in at the O.P. door just before the end. That was for the curtain call.'

'And then everyone came off stage as you expected and in the general movement nobody noticed you'd arrived first.'

'Yes.'

'And you've nothing else to add?'

'There was one thing,' said Niccolini slowly, rather as though he doubted the value of what he was going to say. 'While the applause was still on, it suddenly grew louder for a moment, and then softer again, and I guessed that meant that someone had opened and shut the O.P. door. I did peep round the edge of my door to see if I could see anyone, but there was no one there.'

'There wouldn't have been,' said Searle, 'if the person had gone *on* stage.'

'It was someone,' said Peter. 'But I don't know that that's a very important observation.'

'What are you going to do?' said Martin.

'Nothing. It's not my business. But go now to Mr Pomeroy and tell him what you've told me. He's got a date with the inspector at two o'clock, so you'd better find him at once. If he wants you to tell the police, and I expect he will, I don't think you need worry. They'll forgive you. You see, you do have a little news to tell them.'

Then Davie took an old envelope out of his pocket and wrote a number on it. 'Give me a ring later this afternoon,' he said. 'I would particularly like to know how you get on.'

VIII

It was early for tea when he got back to the Chesterfield, but tea was the thing that he needed and he ordered it.

Willie Marchant (who must have taken a phenomenally long time over his lunch, thought Davie) said, 'Milk? With your views on tea I'd have thought you would have demanded a slice of lemon.'

'No,' said Davie. 'I don't approve of this slice of lemon idea. The result is a form of hot lemonade. People misunderstand that noble fruit. As any cook can tell you, the zest of a lemon lies in the peel. A fragrant curl of peel is as exquisite a thing in your tea-cup as it is in your glass. You don't drink it, you savour it. But you can't expect waiters to waste precious time cutting delicate spirals of lemon peel. So it's milk here, and lemon in Cambridge—but peel, Marchant, peel.'

'So the Russians have been entirely wrong all these years,' said Willie Marchant.

'Good gracious, yes,' said Davie. 'Wrong about so much, but particularly about that.'

'Well,' said Willie Marchant, who was never quite sure when his leg was being pulled, 'I must leave you. I'm late.'

'You should retire, like me,' said Davie. 'Then you can be gloriously late all day.'

There was no one else in the room to talk with. Davie finished his tea, and for a few minutes sat staring at the fender. He was glad that it was an old-fashioned drawing-room fender, and not one of those elevated things on which jolly clubbable men are expected to sit and be merry. He was not feeling merry.

Presently he stirred in his chair and took a thin notebook from his pocket. He took a biro from another pocket and drummed it quietly against his hand for half a minute. Then he began to write.

All my thoughts had been circling about that second DOCTOR. It turns out that it was Martin Searle, having a lark. But nothing is without its value. If Niccolini's story is true two curious things emerge. One is that Tito Adriano went through the O.P. door to reach the stage. He took his call from the other side. Which means he must have walked round behind the scenery. That would account for the white mark on his shoulder. But we do not know how long he stayed on the O.P. side, or why he wanted to go there in the first place.

The other point is Niccolini's story of the apparent opening of the O.P. door after the show had finished. He did not see it open—but he heard the applause grow suddenly louder and then suddenly softer. It is an unmistakable sensation, that: and it is not a thing a man would conveniently invent. He assumed that somebody went on to the stage. But the same effect would have been created by somebody coming off. And that seems to me to be much more likely. The curve of the corridor would account for his not seeing anyone.

So, according to Niccolini, someone (Tito) went on to the stage through the O.P. door—and, a little later, perhaps two minutes later, someone (who?) came off the stage—off, as I think—through the same door. Tito Adriano can confirm or deny the first story. There is no confirmation of the second. And there is no evidence that Niccolini came off the stage as he says he did. He would indeed be gravely suspect if his story did not seem too out of the way to be invented: and it is supported (I do not say confirmed) by Searle. Besides, Niccolini would never have owned up if he knew that doing so would incriminate him.

I accept his story.

Davie drew one of his firm lines across the page, and waited a few seconds, gently prodding his lips with the end of his biro. Then he began to write again.

One thing is certain. Whoever was concerned in this knew exactly what to do, knew exactly when Pantaloon would be alone in the wings—with a minute in which to act, and perhaps three minutes in which to get away. To get away into an empty garden, into the night, into London.

That argues conclusively that the person must have been closely acquainted with the production, must have known where everyone was to an inch and a second. And that means either someone concerned in the show, or someone sufficiently identified with the school routine to be able to watch rehearsals. If sitting at the back of the theatre were too public, there was that little box which Edward Pomeroy used. Pomeroy himself was surely too busy a man to be visiting the box during the day. But anyone else could have used it without being seen.

Then Davie drew another line and underneath it he wrote.

The heart of the matter is contained in three questions.

If Tito Adriano was the murderer, who was the person who came off stage—I think off stage—by the O.P. door?

If the person who came off stage was the murderer, why didn't Tito Adriano see him?

If Niccolini was the murderer, why does he admit to being there?

Then Davie drew another line, closed the notebook, closed his eyes, and relaxed in a gentle dose—from which he was recalled half an hour later by the aged Craddock.

'A telephone call for you, sir—a Mr Searle.'

Davie was immediately awake.

'Thank you. I'll take it.'

'In box one, sir.'

Davie made his way to box one.

'R. V. Davie speaking. How did it go?'

'It was all right. The inspector was a bit grave about giving inaccurate information, but he was interested in what Peter had to tell him.'

'I thought he would be. All is well then?'

'Yes, thank you.'

'There's one thing I would like to ask you,' said Davie. 'I've only just thought of it. When Alan Bastable was found, how was he lying? Do you know?'

'Yes, I do. I was still in the theatre when the S.M. found him. Alan was on his face, legs a bit curled up, but generally back upwards.'

'And he was fully dressed for the part, cloak, mask, and all?'

'He had his cloak on,' said Martin, 'but not the mask—thank

goodness! He'd have looked too horrible in that crafty face. The mask had fallen off. It was lying on the floor beside him.'

'What about his wife? Did she—'

'No. Fortunately she'd gone. She was in a black temper and not attempting to hide it. I'm pretty sure she thought Alan had gone off with Laura. She said she wasn't going to hang around all night and Alan could come home by bus.'

'Poor woman—she'll be regretting that,' said Davie: and then, as Martin Searle made no answer, he went on: 'I presume the police took the clothes and the mask away for examination.'

'I think so, yes.'

'That's what one would expect. I'm glad everything went all right. Goodbye, and thank you for ringing.'

'Goodbye.'

Davie hung up the telephone, and returned slowly to the writing-room. Soon the club would be filling up with evening faces, evening gossip, evening laughter. He hardly thought he could meet any of it. The first part of Martin Searle's conversation had uncovered something he had not known before. He could not interpret it, but he knew that it was important.

Sitting down again in his armchair, he drew his notebook from his pocket and added five more lines.

Alan Bastable was not wearing the Pantaloon mask when he was found. It was lying on the ground beside him.

This is the first significant evidence that I have come across in this extraordinary business.

He was standing in the wings waiting to go on for his call . . .

But there Dr Davie stopped. Before he could go on with that sentence he would have to do a deal more thinking. He put the notebook back in his pocket. It was half past five. At half past six precisely he would get himself a glass of necessary whisky. Till then . . .

Dr Davie shut his eyes and very gratefully returned to his dozing.

Or perhaps he was not dozing. When he stirred in his chair at twenty-five minutes past six he immediately put his hand in his pocket and fished out the notebook again.

Searle said that the mask had fallen off (he wrote) but masks are not made to fall off. And surely, if he were about to go on stage, Alan Bastable wouldn't have been holding it in his hand. The murderer would not have taken it off. What point would there have been in that, and what time had he to lose doing so? Therefore—

I do not see the continuation from "therefore", but unless one of these three suppositions is wrong, there *is* a continuation. There must be.

But the fact was that he had come to the end of an argument. He could see nothing beyond. Besides, no one had asked him to help. Why should he bother?

For a few minutes longer he sat there, staring at the fender. They were old-fashioned indeed, those iron convolutions, like decorations in some book by Aubrey Beardsley. It had probably been there since 1890.

It was a change of subject. Pulling himself out of his chair, he pocketed the notebook and made his way to the bar.

'Six-thirty-*five*,' said George Canteloupe severely. 'I wish you would learn to be punctual, Davie.'

PART THREE

THE RING

Next day Davie went back to Cambridge for the Josiah Brady audit feast, and the college audit feast. These were great occasions, requiring the display of college silver and the observance of several delectable customs. There was the great dish of rose-water, for instance, which was moved down the table part way through dinner. You dipped your napkin in it and dabbed yourself on the lips, the temples, and behind the ears. It was a ritual, but much more than a ritual. There is a nerve behind the ear which rejoices in this refreshment. It works: you can feel it work: it entices you towards the next course. The long clay pipes which were provided at the Josiah Brady feast were less to Davie's taste. These were a survival, the rose-water was an addition to life's pleasures. Besides, the silver dish was itself glorious.

Soon after the feasts it was Christmas, and then the snows came, and the vile February weather. Why he should choose to stay in Cambridge at that time of year Davie could never determine, but he did stay, and when the Lent bumping races came on, he was down on the tow-path, wrapped up to the ears, following the fortunes of St Nicholas's crews.

Never in his life had he pulled that sort of oar, but as a spectator he found the occasion irresistible. He loved that curiously Victorian scene, like some lightly coloured sporting print—the river bank, backed with pollard willows, and the view of the village church on the rising ground beyond the water: and that most amiable of crowds, cheering and laughing, the young men with their girls, the older men without their girls, addicts of the river. And the coaches on bicycles, miraculously weaving along the narrow tow-path, bawling strange exhortations through megaphones. And the boats, so graceful as they paddled to the starting point—but then, transformed, so formidable in pursuit.

If you have planted yourself at the right station on the bank, the excitement of this multiple involvement can be excruciating, for each pursuer is itself pursued, and victory does not come at the winning post, as in a horse race: it comes anywhere—anywhere the pursuing boat can claim a bump, or, conversely, anywhere that the intended victim can make certain of escape. And victory or defeat may be a matter of inches—fluctuating, agonizing inches. Davie, heart in mouth, saw St Nicholas's second boat make a bump, and it made him feel very ill indeed, which, as he told himself on the way home, was highly absurd, because he was not remotely interested in rowing: only in the anxiety of winning by inches.

When the races were over the cold weather retreated, and then, suddenly one day, it was spring, and crocuses lined college avenues. For Davie this was a sign. He decided to go to London. And that same night, in the second week of March, he came back early from dinner and set about packing his suitcase, which was something he did methodically and slowly, because shirts and neckties had to be chosen with grave deliberation. The deep blue tie and the light blue shirt, thought Dr Davie with lamentable vanity; the magenta with the white one; also the pink tie, and the silver.

As he arranged them in his case he remembered the last time he had packed for a visit to London. And the extraordinary happening at the Winston School of Dramatic Art. No doubt the police were still ferreting away at that—but nearly four months had gone by and there had been no arrest. Davie's own thoughts about the crime had advanced not at all. He had heard nothing to advance them. He had stopped thinking about it. But now, here he was, going to London. He would be that much nearer to the mystery. He was secretly aware of an old temptation.

Presently he went into the sitting-room and approached the bookshelves presided over by Letty, his much loved red and white Rockingham cow. And there, with some show of hesitation, he took out the small notebook in which he had recorded the thoughts and speculations of last November.

Standing beside the book-shelves he read the writing through. And yes, he thought, it's a fascinating problem, and even less than usual is it any business of mine.

But he was still holding the notebook when he returned to the bedroom: and presently he tucked it into his suitcase.

There's no offence in that, said Dr Davie deceitfully to his inmost heart.

I I

'You're very quiet these days,' said George Canteloupe two days later, at the Chesterfield club.

'Am I?'

'Yes. What's come over you? You brood, and you ponder.'

'It's not intentional,' said Davie. 'I remember, when young, making a decision—a defensive decision of course—only to speak if I had something worth saying. That didn't last long. The average conversation is entirely worthless, but nothing is gained by withholding from it. Human relationship requires an exchange of words, and so we drivel on. Some of us are aware of our deficiency. Others, and they are the confident ones, are not aware.'

'Well, that's better,' said Canteloupe. 'You are at least drivelling on. What have you been meditating? Your autobiography?'

'Heavens, no! I would never have the vanity to write that. Personal vanity I understand too well. The time and the money I've spent on neckties I would not wish to calculate. But I have no vanity about my life. There would be so much I would regret, so much I would not want to admit. I detest the modern vogue for "telling all". Nowadays autobiographers seem to think it dishonest not to strip to the skin. It may relieve the writer to disburden himself of all the ghastly things he did at his unsavoury little prep school, but why should he shift the burden on to his readers? Only vanity of a very high order can explain this aberration. Besides, the stripper is not entirely candid. He makes a parade of telling all. Sex, he thinks, is welcome—but he does not reveal how he jiggered his income tax or travelled on the underground without paying the proper fare.'

'You are hitting below the belt,' said George Canteloupe.

'I would like to write about the times I have lived in,' Davie went on, 'but not about myself in those times. It is of the deepest interest, I think, that I often saw a muffin man in Chelsea between 1929 and 1939. He carried a tray on his head, covered with a green baize cloth, and he rang a bell. It sounds like Dickens—but only forty years ago that man walked in Chelsea on autumn evenings, *and* rang a bell. There was another man in summer who sold roses. He positively *sang* a line or two about "morning cut roses". This was the nineteen-thirties, Canteloupe, not the eighteenth century. It seems to me that *that* is interesting, but that what I was doing at the time is not. In any case I've forgotten. Autobiography is for politicians and field marshals—people who have something to apologize for.'

'You old devil,' said George Canteloupe. 'You contrived the whole of that speech for the pleasure of saying the last sentence.'

'There *was* a muffin man,' said Davie with dignity. 'And there was a rose man. And now I am going for a walk in a park. There are bulbs popping up all over the place, and they ought to be seen.'

'Furthermore,' said George Canteloupe, his voice pursuing

the retreating Davie, 'you have in no way revealed the reason for your meditations and prolonged silences.'

'Silences!' said Conway Gordon from his accustomed seat by the fireplace. For anyone else to talk at that length was almost an infringement of copyright.

'Silences!'

But Davie did not hear that. He was in the cloakroom struggling into a warm overcoat.

A few minutes later he was on top of a No. 73 bus, bound for Kensington Gardens.

III

The crocuses at Hyde Park Corner had never been more glorious—great slabs of single colours. He might as well have got down there: he would never see anything better. But Hyde Park Corner is a public place. He wanted the old pleasure of being lost among the trees. So he stayed on the bus and went rolling on westwards—past the grand shops of Knightsbridge, past Bowater House, through the arch of which he duly observed that startling back view of the naked family, so eagerly in pursuit of something in the park, sublimely scornful of the law of gravity. And then it was the barracks, and, immediately after, there was the park again.

At the stop before the Albert Hall he got off the bus, crossed the road, and presently entered the great gate which divides the bowls and the bathers and the riders of Hyde Park from the flowers and the babies of Kensington Gardens. There was not a leaf to be seen on the high trees, but the lawns were splashed with gold.

It was not the time of day for pleasant birds. But platoons of pompous pigeons strutted the grass. Davie disliked these boring and voracious creatures. Why, he asked the heavens, do lunatic women encourage them with their horrible bags of stale bread and ancient toast? In general he was in favour of total liberty for everyone, but if there had to be bye-laws, here was a crying call for discipline. There should be a crushing fine for offering pigeons stale bread. Five hundred pounds, say, for the first offence, and three months for the second, to be spent going round with a sack gathering up the repulsive remains. And with the fines, thought Davie, warming to his subject, the Minister of Works could buy millions of lovely bulbs. It was almost worth a letter to *The Times*.

He struck away from the flower walk (the beds trimly waiting the approach of May) and strolled across the grass towards the Round Pond. In the distance he could see the roofs of Kensington Palace and the Orangery. He was always puzzled by orangeries. Had people in the uncentrally-heated seventeenth century really attempted to grow oranges in them? They must have been gravely disappointed.

The palace was looking singularly silent. There were, he remembered, graceful things to look at in the museum. But he was against the famous dolls' house. As a child, he had always questioned the pleasure he was supposed to derive from dolls' houses, trains and motor cars. He had been critical—he clearly remembered being critical—of these frangible imitations which could not be put to any actual enjoyment. A house which unfastened its entire facade was an absurdity, and you could not get into the toy cars and trains either. They were impostures, and Davie had quickly rejected them for the better proportioned pleasures of water and trees. Clearly he was in a minority, the victim, even as a baby, of a distressingly logical turn of mind.

Most people, undoubtedly, are amused by toys. Here, for instance, on the shores of the pond, grown men were seriously engaged in sailing model boats. Overhead the visiting gulls contributed to an illusion of the sea—and, how strange, thought Davie, that the gulls should think it worth their while to fly up from the river to so small a piece of water, that they should even know that it was there. Certainly it was a pretty sight, but the exercise itself seemed tedious.

Near the pond were several elderly gentlemen flying kites. Now if only one could go drifting above the tree tops, attached to a kite by a reliable piece of string, how desirable that would be—better even than floating up a mountain-side on one of those delightful chair-lifts (an entertainment to which Davie was powerfully addicted). But just to stand there unwinding a nylon line, and to watch your kite moored in the sky—that seemed a boring way of spending a spring afternoon. But, ah! beware of pride, and condescension, and opinion! No doubt these parties thought equally poorly of the things that attracted Davie, as he wandered around looking at crocuses, stopping to view football games between large fathers and little sons, observing the strange consortium of dogs, and the lordly prams of expensive babies propelled by genuine nannies: or just watching all the funny people sitting on the benches, looking, as he was looking, at the passing show.

One of these onlookers got up as Davie approached and came to meet him with an enormous smile.

'Martin Searle,' he said. 'Do you remember?'

'Why, yes, of course I do,' said Davie. 'What are you doing here? Why aren't you rehearsing something or other?'

'It's Saturday. We were at it all the morning. You've got to stop sometime.'

'Let's sit,' said Davie. 'Tell me your news. How is your love life?'

'A failure.'

'I'm sorry to hear that. I thought, perhaps, you were going to fix things up with Laura.'

'I did too. But she's got herself engaged to someone else.'

'In the school?'

'No, at the other place—Renton's.'

'Ah.'

'Laura used to be at Renton's, but she got into trouble—with this chap. And Mrs Goode took her away.'

'Mrs Goode?'

'She's her grandmother.'

'I remember, I did hear something about a grand-daughter.'

'It was out of the frying-pan into the fire. All that happened was that Alan Bastable got after her. Laura was like that. There had to be someone. I was only reserve player.'

'And the chap at Renton's didn't give in?'

'He was seeing her all the time. And when Alan went—'

'Persistence was rewarded. What did Mrs Goode think of that?'

'Not much. But she had such a horror of Alan Bastable, who was married and therefore a deceiver, that she now thinks this one's all right. Or almost all right.'

Davie changed the subject. 'How's the acting?' he asked.

'Fine. I've got a good part next week: Flamineo in *The White Devil*—do you know it?'

' "I am i'th'way to study a long silence" ' said Davie. 'No one ever wrote a better line about Death. I hope you're going to remember that the play's written in verse.'

'Will you come to see me?' said Martin. 'It's on every day next week—double cast—I'm doing Monday, Wednesday, Friday.'

A man may sometimes hesitate to put on his coat and stumble out to see some great actor, though the theatre be only round the corner—but surely, any student thinks, not weather nor distance should deter anyone from coming to see him tackle any part in the repertory, however unsuitable. The expectation is unreasonable, but it is also endearing. Davie could not possibly have refused.

'Certainly I'll come.'

'It must be Monday, Wednesday, or Friday.'

Davie took out his engagement book. 'Monday. Monday's all right. What do I do?'

'Just come. You can get seats at the door. I think they're five bob,' said Martin colouring a little. 'Perhaps they'll give me one.'

'Don't bother. It's a good cause. Five bob: that used to be such an agreeable round sum. I can't take kindly to twenty-five new pence, can you?'

Davie paused a moment to consider an old lady and a dowager spaniel. They were of an age. 'Come along, Floss,' said the old lady. But Floss stood still, lifting her white nose towards the water, sniffing perhaps old splashes on the margin of the pond, and sticks, and balls bouncing along the turf. 'Floss!' said the old lady, a little sternly, and Floss, with a gentle movement of her stern, the merest memory of a wag, continued slowly round the path. They would be a long time getting home.

'You haven't made any mention of the events of last November,' said Davie.

'That's because there's nothing to say. The police were all over the place for days, photographing things and taking measurements and hunting for fingerprints, and interviewing people. But they never made any sense of it—which suggests—'

'That it was done by someone outside the school.'

Martin Searle nodded his head. 'That's just it. Anyone could have got into the back of the theatre that night. Absolutely anyone.'

'And got away before the audience did?'

'If it had all been worked out to a cunning time-table.'

'That's the point. Was that possible?' said Davie, remembering, even as he spoke, the car which disappeared down the drive into the London night.

'Even if it wasn't possible,' said Martin, 'I suppose he could have mingled with the crowd.'

'Yes,' said Davie. 'I suppose so.' Though somehow he did not feel that that was a very likely explanation.

For half a minute neither of them said anything. Then, 'By the way, what happened to Bastable's wife?' Davie asked.

'Harriet.'

'Yes.'

'She left the school.'

'That's understandable.'

'She made a great fuss because Alan's ring was missing. It was valuable. Or she said it was: which isn't quite the same thing. It wasn't insured, which is odd if it *was* valuable. She said he used to wear it on the stage, and Michael Teed, who dressed with him, confirmed that. He says it was a big ruby-looking stone, but Alan never said it was real, and naturally Michael assumed it was a bit of stage jewellery out of Mrs Goode's glory box.'

'And was it?'

'Mrs Goode says no. Most people believed it was a lot of talk.'

'But if it had been a real ruby, one might begin to smell a motive.'

'Yes—but how do you prove a thing like that? How can you be sure he did wear it that night?'

'He wore *a* ring,' said Davie. 'I remember it. And it was red.'

'He didn't have one when he was found.'

'Did you notice that yourself?'

'No—I didn't notice a thing. But the police take inventories. If there'd been a ring it would have been noted, and Harriet would have got it back.'

'So the assumption is that the murderer took the ring?'

'That's Harriet's assumption.'

'And the ring might therefore have been the reason for the murder?'

'Yes.'

'H'm,' said Davie. There was nothing more to say about that.

After a short pause he asked, 'Is Tito still at the school?'

'No, he isn't. I suppose he didn't feel like doing another *commedia* play on that stage.'

'And I don't suppose Edward Pomeroy wanted one either.'

'Edward was quite ill after that business. He had to go away before the end of term. And Mrs Goode was ill, too, for the first time in living memory. She'd got herself into a state because she would have it that someone got into the wardrobe after she left that night. Apparently there was a Pantaloon costume at the end of a rack, and next to it a Doctor's costume.'

'Yes,' said Davie, 'I happen to remember that.'

'Well, when she got in next day—rather late, because the police wouldn't let anyone in for a bit—she found that the Doctor's dress had been moved. It was at the end of the rack.'

'Was this anything to do with you?'

'No, no: I had my own costume.'

'Was there anything wrong with this wardrobe dress?'

'I don't think so—but Mrs Goode says that someone must have taken it and put it back in the wrong place. What do you make of that?'

'At first thought,' said Davie, 'I make three Doctors. You, Niccolini and X.'

'Yes.'

'But, at second thought, I think that's being rather simpleminded. Had the place been broken into?'

'No, it hadn't.'

'One would have guessed that Mrs Goode might be mistaken. Did she report this?'

'I think not. She doesn't like policemen. I think she was only cross because she thought someone had been fiddling with her clothes.'

'I see.'

'Then she got ill. Laura had to look after her. Priscilla had to do the wardrobe: it was chaos.'

'Oh dear,' said Davie, but not with reference to the chaos.

Hopeful that he had spotted a sucker, a Labrador puppy had sidled up and laid an ancient tennis ball at his feet. Here was a familiar problem of the Gardens. To refuse those trusting eyes would be flinty-hearted: to accept would be to enchain oneself to charity. Davie enchained himself. He threw the ball.

'I saw Tito the other day,' said Martin. 'He still lives quite close. He said he was doing a *commedia* show at Renton's."

'Oh?' said Davie in as level a tone as he could muster. 'When is this?'

The Labrador puppy, confidently returning, was abashed to find himself ignored.

'It's been on since Wednesday. Tonight's the last night. Do you want to see it?'

Davie looked down his nose. More than anything he wanted to see it. He had never hoped for such another opportunity. But he only said, 'That might be interesting. Supposing I went, what would I have to do?'

'Just roll up. There'll be seats.'

'Time?'

'Seven-thirty.'

'And Renton's is—'

'Notting Hill Gate. I'll write it down.'

Martin drew a rough map on the back of an envelope. 'There you are.'

'Thank you,' said Davie, getting up. 'I must be getting back now. It's none too warm sitting. I'm sorry, dog. Goodbye. I'll see you on Monday.'

'You won't forget?'

'Cross my heart,' said Davie lightly. But as he went down the Broad Walk his head was filled with dazzling thoughts. Unbelievably he had a chance to see those masks a second time: and a fair and proper reason to visit the Winston School again. At that moment he was no wiser than he was four months before. But opportunity seemed to beckon. To Renton's and to Winston Manor he would most certainly go.

When he reached the high road he looked back towards Bayswater, raising its terracotta domes at the far end of the Broad Walk. It looked like a glimpse of Byzantium.

And then a 73 bus came up, and he climbed to the top deck, and so returned by easy stages to the eighteenth century.

IV

Getting to Renton's in time to secure a seat would mean leaving the club at a quarter to seven: and what about dinner? Better, Davie thought, to leave at a quarter to six. There was an agreeable Italian restaurant at the top of Kensington Church Street. And so (after lying down on his bed and making up stories about the ladies and gentlemen on his toile de Jouy wall-paper till he dropped asleep) he turned his face that way, boarding an 88 bus in Oxford Street just after the worst of the homeward traffic was over. In his pocket he carried a stopwatch borrowed from Alfred, the junior hall porter. Davie knew a mysterious lot about other people's interests. He had long known that Alfred, who was lean and leggy, was an amateur of the track, and given to running round Hyde Park in shorts at an early hour in the morning. And so, 'Lend me a stop-watch,' he had confidently asked, and Alfred had said he would do that with pleasure, adding a wealth of detail about the use of stop-watches and the extraordinary accomplishment of the split second.

It was not a subject which had heretofore engaged the attention of Dr Davie, but he had managed to profess a suitable interest, and was presently rewarded. 'That way to start, that way to stop, and push the winder to get it back to zero again?' 'You've got it, sir,' said Alfred. 'I was not proposing positively to run round Hyde Park myself.' 'Was you not, sir?' said Alfred. They had had a good laugh over that.

Dead in the eye of the setting sun the 88 bus travelled, past

Marble Arch, which is not made of marble, past Tyburn, that scene of blood, and past masses more of crocuses, though here the colours were too freely mixed. They are best in blocks, crocuses. And so, the park on the left, the stately houses on the right, they came to Bayswater, which, at close quarters, is as little like Byzantium as anything might be, being largely composed of enormous pillared Victorian squares, not really in decay, but totally out of fashion—indeed, these days, almost a foreign settlement, so many are the languages, so many the swarthy un-English sorts of men, hailing from Italy to South America.

Renton's School of Dramatic Art, as Davie was presently to discover, was contained within three of these houses thrown together. Huge houses they were, five floors above ground and one below, family houses never again to be occupied by one family, never again to know a staff of uniformed servants, never again to have coal fires in the bedrooms, factories for that famous London fog, long since departed.

The place was a warren, a puzzle. Rooms had been run together, cut in half, screwed around, and the whole complex honeycombed with steps and passages. But by doggedly navigating a number of straits and hopefully investigating a variety of stairs, he found himself eventually at the entrance to the theatre, which had been erected in the combined gardens of the three houses.

It was a very different building from that at Winston Manor. It was oblong, had to be oblong, and was therefore irredeemably "proscenium". But if the shape were old-fashioned the customers were the reverse. This audience had no Mrs Pheasants, no Miss Mannerings, no Mrs Torrianos out on the spree. Rather, these were people connected with the theatre, friends of the actors, friends of friends, their conversation a little more shrill, a little more sophisticated, than the tattle of North London.

Davie retired into a corner of the small foyer and studied the programme. As he had hoped, it was the same play, and, from the cast, it looked like being the same after-piece. For scholarly reasons it would be enormously interesting to compare the performances. For other reasons—well, he could not tell, but his hand closed round the stop-watch in his pocket.

Voices drifted to his ears.

'Have you been to *The Less the Merrier*?'

'No—have you? I hear it's terribly amusing.'

'It's staggering. It's all done in reverse. The bedroom scene is fully clothed. Bowlers, my dear! But in the drawing-room, that's act two, everyone's completely starkers.'

'Golly! And how's the dialogue?'

'That's thin, deliberately thin. Amy was writing for the eye. And I think she was right. One must have a focus.'

A bell rang.

'Of course it won't get any further than Tottenham Court Road.'

People began to move into the theatre.

'Do you know what this is about?' said somebody.

'I think it's a masque.'

'Oh.'

A minute later the curtain—for Renton's Theatre was sufficiently unenlightened to have such a thing—rose upon *Il Pellegrino Fido Amante*: "The faithful pilgrim lover"—it was rather a mouthful in English.

As Davie had expected, he was captivated all over again by the masks. It was possible, he supposed, that they might be badly managed, but, provided the parts were played reasonably well, it was the masks which created the sport. In this kind of work, indeed, it must be harder for the women: they have to act with their own faces.

Davie found himself watching Pantaloon in particular. He would hardly have known he was watching a different actor, so nearly the same was the mask and the clothes, and the business. This chap, too, wore a great ruby-coloured ring, as

Alan Bastable had done. If Martin Searle had not spoken about the alleged loss of Bastable's ring Davie might not have noticed the presence of this one. But now it focused his attention. Was a ruby-looking ring traditional in the part? It was interesting. Suddenly, for once in a way, he felt a powerful desire to go behind after the show, to meet these actors. But how to manage that, he was thinking as he made his way out of the auditorium at the end of the first play. He had no conceivable excuse.

'Bother it,' said Dr Davie, entering the foyer—and the next moment halted, astonished at the favour of fortune. There, in a corner, admirably posed before a basket of mauve tulips, was Tito Adriano, and alone.

Dr Davie did not hesitate. 'May I be so bold as to introduce myself to you, Mr Adriano,' he said.

'Please,' said Tito with a courtly inclination of his handsome head.

'My name is Davie, and I am very interested in anything to do with the *commedia dell'arte*. I saw your production at the Winston School last November and enjoyed it enormously.'

'I am so glad.'

'So, when I heard news of this production, I was anxious to see your work again. It's a form of entertainment that fills me with delight. It's a basic joke. It's the mirror of all humour.'

'I am very happy,' said Tito. 'Thank you so much. The actors will be pleased to know.'

And there it was. 'Could I have the pleasure of telling them so myself?' said Davie.

'Yes, indeed. After the show I will take you round with pleasure,' said Tito Adriano, turning at the same time to acknowledge a stoutish man with a shining countenance who was bearing down on them with an alarming show of cordiality.

'This is Mr—' began Tito.

'Davie.'

'Davie. May I introduce the director, Mr Male.'

A singularly inappropriate name, thought Davie, as he said 'How do you do?'

But Mr Male was not one for empty formalities. 'How very good of you to come,' he cried, seizing Davie by the hand in an ecstasy of welcome.

As Touchstone grades the tones of a retort, so one might grade the various kinds of handshake. Besides the handshake proper, which is firm, short, and true, there is the handshake limp, and the handshake wet, both of which deny the intention of greeting; the grip intolerable, which is an uninvited demonstration of masculinity; the reinforced handshake, which, by bringing a second hand to the support of formality, successfully establishes a certainty of insincerity; and, last, the handshake prolonged, the grip that will not let you go. It is accompanied by warm words and warm looks, and it turns the heart to ice. This is the most hard to bear of all.

It was the handshake of Mr Male.

'Mr Davie,' said Tito, 'is a student of the *commedia dell-'arte.*'

'He is!' said Mr Male, withdrawing a little in simulated astonishment, but still gripping on to Davie's hand. 'How very delightful!'

'With your permission I am going to introduce him to our actors.'

'But, of course, my dear fellow. Do do that. I am absolutely delighted. The actors will be delighted. We are all—I'm so sorry,' said Mr Male, suddenly releasing Davie. 'Do forgive me, but I absolutely must speak to Dame Margaret. So very good of you to come.'

Mr Male had seen someone else who needed greeting.

'God help us,' said Davie, under his breath.

'When it is over,' said Tito, 'come to the front of the auditorium. I will meet you at the curtain. That is the easiest way through.'

V

There was none of the up-to-date luxury of the Winston School at Renton's. Mr Male could not have said with Mr Pomeroy, 'In its humble way it's like the opera house at Vienna.' Behind the stage there were two dressing-rooms and that was all, one for the boys, one for the girls.

Tito led Davie into the men's department. Round two sides of the room ran a narrow continuous table, carrying trays of grease paint, cleaning rags, masks, winking theatrical jewels, wrist watches, combs, all sorts of bits and pieces, doubling themselves in the continuous looking-glass behind the table. And sitting at the table were some eight young men in various stages of undress, one in a shirt, three in vests, the others in next to nothing, simultaneously presenting their backs and their reflected faces to visitors. It would have made, thought Davie, a marvellous subject for a French painter round about 1900.

There was a curious, not unpleasant, fug in the room, compounded of grease paint, soap, and chaps.

'Here is a visitor,' said Tito. 'This is Mr Davie and he knows about the *commedia*.'

'I've only come round to say thank you,' said Davie, 'and to tell you how much I've enjoyed your performance.' At which welcome remark faces turned round, or smiled back at him from the looking-glasses. Nobody dislikes praise and actors notoriously live upon it.

'Of course I haven't the least idea which of you was which.'

'This is the Doctor,' said Tito. 'That's the Captain. Brighella's over there. Also Harlequin. And this monster is Pantaloon.'

'Tell me,' said Davie, 'is there anything traditional about Pantaloon wearing a big red stone on his finger?'

'I don't think so,' said Adriano.

'I ask because this chap had a whopping great ring tonight—and the last Pantaloon I saw wore one too. So I wondered.'

Nestling behind a chunk of cotton wool, the ring shone back at him in the looking-glass, square-cut, bright red, set in gilt—it seemed absurd to suppose gold.

And behind the ring in the glass, the young man. About twenty-five. Dark hair upon his chest. Strong. Handsome. Sexy. And, for some private reason, blushing.

'I've seen a Pantaloon with a ring,' he said. 'I thought it looked good. So I copied him.'

'Actors adore jewellery,' said Tito. 'That's what they like about seventeenth-century drama. They can wear a ring on each finger. But I never heard that a ring was an essential part of Pantaloon's costume.'

'It would be interesting to study the pictures.'

'I've got a lot of pictures,' said Tito. 'You should come to see them some time.'

'I'd like to very much,' said Davie. 'Well, I mustn't keep you, gentlemen. I only wanted to say thank you. I love this sort of humour, and I thought you did it splendidly. Good night.'

'Good night.' 'Thank you.' 'Good night.'

'I'll see you to the door,' said Tito.

'Good heavens, no! Please don't bother.'

'Oh yes: you'll have to go out the back way. You don't know where it is.'

'I forgot that.'

'Mind the step.'

'There are a great many steps ripe for the minding in this building. It's like some hermit's grotto cut in the living rock.'

'Here it is,' said Tito, but paused with his hand on the door-knob. 'The other ring you were thinking of,' he said, 'was Alan Bastable's, wasn't it? The chap who played the part at Winston. You know, of course, that he was killed.'

'Yes.'

'It's a funny thing—they never found that ring. It just

vanished. But what was the point in stealing a bit of theatre jewellery?'

'None at all. I therefore conclude that there was a different reason for its disappearance.'

'You think so?'

'What else can one think? That sort of thing doesn't happen by accident.'

'I suppose not.'

'Thank you again so much. You have been most kind and I have been most interested.'

'Thank you. If you ever want to see my pictures, do let me know.'

'I will. Thank you. Good night.'

It was a four-minute walk to the bus stop. It had been raining a little and the roads shone in the lamplight. It was extraordinary, thought Davie, how empty a side street could be at night. Queensway might be full of people, but this street was deserted, silent: flanked with curtained windows occasionally betraying a crack of light. It was like a street in a film set, frightening if it were not for the comforting red buses which, every now and then, floated across the far end. That was where he had to go: the Bayswater Road.

But these were dramatic emotions. He did not really think illwishers were lurking in the shadows: and very soon his thoughts were back in Renton's Theatre, reviewing the events of the last two hours.

He had wanted to meet the actors because he had wanted to see the ring. But the ring had told him nothing. There had been no point in seeing it. Two Pantaloons had worn a red ring. It was mildly interesting, but if you could not identify the first ring, the second was without significance.

The odd thing about his visit had been something totally unexpected. He had seen this Pantaloon before. And he knew where. This was the young man with the suitcase, the young man Adriano had spoken to in the foyer at the Winston

Theatre: the young man who had told his companion that he wasn't staying for the second half of the show. If that meant anything he had no idea what it was: but even a bit of sky in the top corner contributes something to a jigsaw puzzle. Mentally he dropped it into place.

It was not very warm. Turning his collar up, and putting his hands in his overcoat pockets, he was immediately reminded that he carried something hard and round in the right hand pocket of his jacket. The stop-watch. He had gone to the theatre particularly in the hope of seeing the second piece. And he had been rewarded. So far as he could remember, the knockabout had been played in much the same way as at the Winston Theatre, four months before. But then he had sat alone. Tonight he had been accompanied by a relentlessly accurate witness.

Forty seconds. As theatrical evidence it must be true, though hardly believable. As criminal evidence—it was surely destructive of an accepted theory. It detected an impossibility.

When Davie got back to the Chesterfield Club he went first to his bedroom, where he collected his notebook, and then to the library. At this hour of night, when the rooms were full of men that he knew, to sit downstairs studying a notebook would be highly unclubbable (Dr Johnson's devastating adjective for poor Sir John Hawkins). He needed to think, and he thought best with a pen in his hand.

As he expected, there was no one in the library. He sat down in a leather-covered armchair by the fire. Not so long ago it would have been a cheerful coal fire. Now it was electric, and the fools had closed the chimney in, so that there was no circulation of air. It wouldn't be long before the bindings on the books began to crack, the joins in the fine furniture to come unstuck, the marquetry on the table in the window to unfasten itself like some puzzle which hadn't been played with for two hundred years. We were the cleaner for it, no doubt, and the healthier, he grudgingly supposed, but alas, it was not so comfortable as it used to be, it was not so beautiful.

Dr Davie opened his notebook and began to write without hesitating for a word.

The thing that is so baffling is the time factor. Bastable could not have been killed until after Clown had entered to make his bow. Whether Clown saw Tito, or whether he didn't, makes no difference. According to the stop-watch there were only forty seconds between Clown's entry from the O.P. side and Tito's entry from the Prompt side. It was seventy seconds to the end of the applause and the last curtain. At the Winston Theatre it could have been a little longer: there was that incident when Clown dusted Tito down with his feather brush. Say eighty seconds.

This means that, if Tito did it, he had only forty seconds to stab, cover up the body, and get round to the other side. It would perhaps be possible. But who would be so sanguine as to bank upon it?

If someone other than Tito did it—Niccolini, or anyone who had managed to conceal themselves on the stage—that person would have had, say, eighty seconds to stab, cover up, and escape. This is a little easier, and, according to Niccolini's evidence, someone almost certainly did leave the stage during the applause. It could not have been a member of the cast. They were all on stage.

But *eighty* seconds—at most eighty seconds. It is hard to accept—and yet there are the facts. A man comes off the stage alive. Forty, fifty, sixty seconds later he is dead, stabbed in the back.

And there Davie suddenly stopped. What rubbish he was writing! Facts! *Facts?* That is what one tells oneself. He was found there, so he was killed there. But obviously he *could* have gone off anywhere—an empty dressing-room, the loo, or even outside the theatre altogether. He *could* have been killed wherever he happened to be, and he could have been hidden on the stage after the cast had left—except the S.M. and Martin Searle.

Oh God! said Davie to himself. This thinking is good because it shows that there could be an explanation other than the accepted one—but I dislike the way it leads me. I can't turn away from Tito and Niccolini to suspect that pleasant young man, Searle. I reject the consequence of my own argument. Very well, then, I must find something else I do believe.

He returned to his notebook.

Alan Bastable *could* have been killed during the final curtains. I no longer believe this. The stop-watch has destroyed that theory for me. The idea that he was killed *afterwards* is far more acceptable from the point of time and opportunity—but it is full of obvious difficulties. How could he have been brought back to the stage without anyone seeing? And what would the point be of bringing him back to the stage? He could have been found anywhere.

Therefore—what?

That what is the answer.

Add to these problems the problem of the ring. Why did it disappear? Why did Harriet say it was valuable when everyone else, including Tito (interesting, that), believed that it wasn't?

Add—I suppose it should be added—Mrs Goode's rather misty agitation about someone messing about with the Doctor's costume. Why the *Doctor's* costume? This seems meaningless to me. Apparently her only complaint was that the costume was out of position. It hadn't been damaged or obviously used. It was out of place. She liked things just so, and they weren't. I think she got caught up in the general excitement and imagined things.

At which point Davie suddenly stopped writing and stared across the room at the book-shelves.

In his mind he was seeing a picture of Mrs Goode, as he had seen her that November evening, back to the window, electric iron in hand, the full racks of clothes, stretching away from her on either side in avenues, and the shorter rack, the largely depleted *commedia* rack—Columbine, the Doctor, Pantaloon. He remembered the whole scene so well—Pomeroy miming the part of the Doctor, and Mrs Goode's parting remark, 'You'd make a lovely Doctor, dear, with your legs.' The room had been in the trimmest possible shape: and certainly Mrs Goode was the kind of person who would know exactly where everything was. But, 'Of course,' said Davie suddenly out loud, 'she might have been looking at things the wrong way round!'

It was a strange remark, and Davie seemed so surprised at what he heard himself saying that he sat there bolt upright for half a minute, his lips parted, his eyebrows raised. Then, 'In that case,' he whispered, 'in that case ... the mask ... and the ring—the position of the mask—and the absence of the ring, could make sense, equal sense.'

Staring at the bookcases, Dr Davie sat on in the library for another thirty minutes. But he wrote no more in his notebook.

VI

Two days are an awful long time to wait for something important. He returned Alfred's stop-watch. He fiddled with the Sunday papers. He began Sally Antrobus's latest—*A Cloistered Death*. He liked Sally Antrobus, but he could not settle his mind on the goings-on in the Cathedral Close at Muncaster. Always his own problem overlay whatever he was reading. At the Archdeacon's fatal garden party, Mr Male was in the background, indefatigably shaking hands with a Rural

Dean. Softly exploring the cathedral in one of Miss Antrobus's most creepy scenes, he passed quite close to Mrs Goode, whispering with Mr Pomeroy in a dim moonlit chapel: 'You'd make a lovely Doctor, dear, with your legs'. Miss Pringle, and Tito Adriano, mixed with the crowds in the market square. In the window glass of a shop in Muncaster High Street he saw the face of that young man at Renton's—indeed more than the face, for he saw him as he had seen him in the dressing-room glass, naked, hairy, sexy and blushing.

There was nothing to be gained by thinking about his problem. At the moment there was nothing new to think. But the subject would not let him be. Even when George Canteloupe joined him in the writing-room it was the subject that commanded the conversation.

'George, give me your advice,' said Davie. 'Not counting gangsters who do it for revenge and for terror: not counting maniacs: what is most likely to compel an ordinary person towards premeditated murder. Not anger, that's unpremeditated. Is it Hate? Or Lust? Or Jealousy? Or Greed?'

George Canteloupe settled himself into a deep chair and considered.

'I don't think an *ordinary* person ever commits murder—but of those four Hate is last. Hate turns people up, leads them the other side of the street. Hate like Pizzaro's in *Fidelio* doesn't exist in real life. I'd say Greed comes first. Think of all those wives who have poisoned their husbands for a small independence.'

'Think of Smith and his baths.'

'Jealousy and Lust are equals. Protecting one's own or snatching somebody else's own.'

'And a mixture of Greed with either one of them would be ahead of anything.'

'Yes.'

'I am glad to have your opinion.'

'You are, I presume, on one of your safaris?'

'I'm puzzling over something that worries me. It's none of my business—'

'Naturally not.'

'But it is rewarding when one can make things fit.'

'Like crosswords.'

'Not like crosswords. I can't do crosswords. Crosswords are artificial. Sometimes I get the word and still don't understand the clue. In the sort of puzzle that interests me, the clue springs from human behaviour. The jocosities of a verbal juggler do not. Maybe I do jigsaws. I don't do crosswords.'

'I sit corrected,' said Canteloupe, but added, 'You left out one category, you old fool.'

'What's that?'

'The preventive murder. The chap who murders the man with the evidence.'

'You're right. He's high. High as Greed. But Greed comes before Love.'

'Does Love come into it? Jealousy and Lust aren't Love.'

'Aren't they?'

'You speak very innocently, R.V.'

'I am extremely innocent, George. That, surely, is well known to my friends—limited though their circle regrettably is.'

Davie had talked himself round to a smile. In the afternoon he took himself off to the Victoria and Albert Museum. There were two exhibitions he wanted to see, "The Treasures of Althorp" and "The Ethiopian Tradition". These, he hoped, would engage the mind.

Pictures and furniture, gold, silver and china, the treasures superbly represented the best creations of a formal age: but how alike the ladies were in their gold frames and how faultless all the carpentry. In those surroundings a tiny rose chipped from a Meissen plate seemed an unpardonable impropriety. How different was the tradition of Ethiopia!

Those people painted what they saw, as best they could, painted it flat and painted it true.

Particularly remarkable was the scene of the Christian King Theodore administering justice. Before the Lion of Judah sat his court, and a little beyond their circle the malefactors were suffering the immediate execution of their punishments. The happiest four were dangled from a tree. Another wrapped in waxed linen was blazing as a torch. One was being stoned, another having his tongue cut out, another losing a foot, another an eye. Another was being flogged, another branded. And in the corner stood three men in fetters, awaiting His Majesty's word. Flat and crude, no brush of Van Dyck or Joshua Reynolds ever matched the expression in those eyes. And God! thought Davie, here am I, troubling myself with a murder by a humane and instant method: and there was King Theodore in the name of Christian justice punishing small law-breakers with lingering savagery. Theodore, Ivan the Terrible, Ali Pasha, Stalin, Papa Doc, the Mafia . . . Henry VIII boiled a man in oil—a cook accused of trying to poison Sir Thomas More. But when the horrible Howard woman, Kerr's wife, undoubtedly did poison Sir Thomas Overbury, James I let her live. She was a person of quality. Let justice be done is an easy empty saying. Whether it is or not, the heavens will not fall. So why should I think it necessary to discover who killed Alan Bastable? Do I want justice done? I do not. I only want to exercise my mind. To be right! It is a mean and vain desire.

Deeply depressed, he passed the glass revolving doors and stayed a moment on the museum steps to watch the passing scene. So many tongues and shades of countenance there were, so many map-readers, sadly studying the inconsequence of London.

In the square across the road forsythia blazed in one corner: in another an almond tree was nearly in flower. On a huge hoarding to the right a vast advertisement proclaimed the cool joys of somebody's cigarettes. If they brought in a law enforcing the printing of a warning on cigarette packets, would it apply to posters too?

SOANDSO'S CIGARETTES
ARE
COOL, SWEET
AND
DEADLY

It was a pleasant thought.

But, on the top of his homeward bus the Ethiopian tradition returned to vex him. He was obliged to concentrate on Alan Bastable to drive King Theodore away.

VII

Monday was a different day. Monday has shops, crowded pavements, roads jammed with cars and buses. Monday one has to keep one's wits about one.

Davie visited his tailor. There still are such people. The great collections of reach-me-downs have not entirely obliterated this distinguished craft. And since the tailor is an old-fashioned delight, he remains, and consciously remains, an Edwardian, almost a Dickensian, figure.

Davie liked going to his tailor. It was an exercise in decorum. Discussing points of dress with Mr Thankful was serious work, by no means to be hurried. But eventually the number and the posting of the cuff buttons was agreed, the zip preferred to the fly ('The zip,' said Mr Thankful, 'is readier to the hand') and the hip pocket rejected as unnecessary, dangerous, and unfashionable.

'We will send you a card when we are ready,' said Mr

Thankful, conducting Davie to the door with professional courtesy.

Davie always flinched from saying thank you to Mr Thankful. He had suffered a similar neurosis when writing to a certain Mr Dear. 'Dear Dear' had been almost unspellable. But such things have to be faced and so 'Thank you very much, Mr Thankful,' said Davie, and stepped into the sunlight.

Crossing the Haymarket and Lower Regent Street, he made his way to St James's Square, bound for the London Library. There Time remains outside on the pavement. 1880, 1910, 1930: in this most restful place the furniture, the manners, and indeed sometimes the clothes, suggest any time in the courteous past rather than the hastening present. Everyone moves and speaks quietly here. Davie desired the complete works in one volume of Ronald Firbank, and a forgotten play by a forgotten author. There was not the slightest difficulty about that.

The third good thing a man can do on a free morning is to visit his barber, and that way Davie now bent his steps like one predestined.

When Dr Davie went to the barber he always stayed a long time, for a hair-cut meant also firm hands on the face, hot towels, cold towels, deep scented creams, stinging astringent lotions, and wayward hairs yanked out between the eyebrows, for as No. 19 frequently remarked, it would never do if Dr Davie were drowned at sea.

A barber's shop is a hall of mirrors. As you sit in your chair you command a vista of reflected heads, some crowned with towels, some creamed with soap, old gentlemen bowing bald domes over basins, small surpliced boys, like choristers uplifted on adjustable thrones, their mothers scanning *Punch* and *Country Life* in the ante-room. But when it comes to massaging and towelling, the client must be tilted backward. Davie lay back, outstretched, and stared at the inside of a towel, while No. 19 stood behind him pressing its heat against his cheeks, against his eyes, till colours flashed across the darkness. The hot towels were stifling, the cold towels made him gasp, stabbing him in the vitals like a knife. It was the same feeling as he got when he peered over the side of a high bridge. But, hot or cold, it was an exhilarating entertainment.

I might be an embalmed mummy, he was thinking. I am swathed from head to knee, unrecognizable except for shoes and trouser ends, the tip of my nose, and, I suppose, a shock of hair. I might be anyone, as Harlequin or the Doctor or the Captain might be anyone but for extremities. You'd make a lovely Doctor, dear, with your legs. A lovely Harlequin, dear, with—he supposed—your hands. A lovely Pantaloon—but then No. 19 tilted the chair upright, and there he was again in the glass, and prompted instantly to complete his sentence. A lovely Pantaloon, dear, thought Dr Davie, with your hair.

No. 19 combed it down over his eyes, doused it with a lilac spirit, searched for the parting, made it once, then combed it down again and had a second go. This was a ritual of perfection, akin, Davie thought, to that ceremonial making of tea in the East, when the host casts away the first brew as unworthy, and exercises his art a second, or even a third, time, earnest to achieve, or seem to achieve, the pink of hospitality.

But the parting made, there, finally, he was, boiled, refrigerated, polished, and sleek. No. 19 dusted him down with a little powder, and wiped it off again, handed a sacramental towel to dab against his cheek, then stood aside, clothes-brush in hand, awaiting his uprising. Four token sweeps with the brush, and they accompanied each other to the cash desk, where No. 19 asked Davie if he wanted anything else, and Davie said no thank you, he didn't (though that was not precisely true) and thus they parted, with cordial thanks on both sides. It was half past twelve.

Davie walked back to the club. Naturally he did. He was feeling ten years younger—an illusion which persisted for a full twenty minutes. And as he walked he saw himself again in the barber's chair, swathed like a mummy, saw others too, masked, towelled, disguised: which so put him in mind of his reflections on Saturday night that he resolved to get to Winston Manor a little early that evening.

Before the play, indeed before dinner, if it could be discreetly managed, he meant to pay a call on Mrs Goode.

VIII

It was a quarter past five when he reached the gates of Winston Manor. Mr Pomeroy had certainly done well with the garden. The drive was lined with daffodils. Forsythia stood gold among the evergreens. In the distance three almond trees were posed like a Japanese print. Nearer the house, in small round beds, were two deep red camellias.

It was Davie's plan to walk up the drive and turn firmly to the right, down the path to the main door of the theatre. His excuse was the box office. If it were open he would buy a ticket. But probably it would not be open. In which event, if anyone were about, he would regret having made a mistake and make amiable enquiries about the show. But if no one were about, he intended to slip through the door into the corridor. And once there, he would walk boldly along to the wardrobe. He felt sure Mrs Goode would be pleased to see him.

The trouble was passing the house. He did not want to be involved either with Mr Pomeroy or with Miss Pringle. The best thing was not to look at the house. If they did see him, said Davie to himself, carefully bending his glance to the gravelled path, they wouldn't recognize him. Anyway his intentions were admirable. He wanted a ticket, and he was going to pay for it.

The box office was not open. Nor was there anyone in the foyer, though he could hear voices in the auditorium. The producer was fussing with the lighting. A first night is never quite ready till it's begun. And not always then, thought Davie, remembering how Sheridan had written the last scene of *Pizzaro* after the rise of the curtain, and handed it out on bits of paper to those remarkable Kembles.

He opened the swing door and entered the corridor.

The canteen was not yet open, but through the round glass window he could see an attendant nymph making ready for the evening, at the instant (he uselessly observed) assembling a dish of hard-boiled eggs on the counter.

Guiltily he hurried on down the corridor. With so many witnessing half-open doors, it seemed a long way to the wardrobe.

Mrs Goode was standing in exactly the same position as that in which he first beheld her—back to the window, iron in hand, intent on somebody's frilled shirt, the centre point in a perspective of costumes.

'May I come in?' said Davie. 'I don't suppose you remember me.'

'Oh yes I do, dear,' said Mrs Goode. 'I never forget faces. Mr Pomeroy brought you in last November.'

'He did. I am coming to the show this evening—and I thought I'd do myself the pleasure of calling on you.'

'I remember your coming very well,' said Mrs Goode, her mind still on the previous November. 'It was the night that Alan Bastable died.'

Davie had received his cue sooner than expected. He said, 'No one ever settled that mystery, did they?'

'No. And I don't suppose now they ever will.'

'Did you know Alan Bastable well?'

'Of course, dear,' said Mrs Goode. 'I know all of them well. And I knew *him* only too well. I shouldn't speak ill of the dead, but he was a wicked young man, and that's the truth. He was a married man, you know, and he spent all his time running after the young girls. That was the trouble. And I wouldn't be surprised if that wasn't at the bottom of what happened.'

Mrs Goode smoothed the shirt once again, more as a pause-filling gesture than a necessity, folded it neatly across and laid it on the end of the table. Davie waited. And presently, as he expected, Mrs Goode continued. 'He was an orphan, and that was partly it, I dare say. He was brought up by an aunt—and that's not the same thing at all, dear. I saw her once at a production. Stuffy-looking woman. Miss Florence Bastable. I suppose she was his father's sister. When she died last year it turned out she'd been living on an annuity. Which didn't help to keep Alan on terms with his wife. And *she's* no good either, in my opinion,' said Mrs Goode, turning to search for something in a rack of garments proper for high persons of the sixteenth century. 'I dare say he had a lot to put up with, but he was a wicked young man for all that.'

Returning to her base by the window, Mrs Goode shook out an elaborately jewelled cloak, and attempted to change the subject. 'It's nice, isn't it?' she said. 'The Duke of Venice. That's next week, and they're doing it in the proper period.'

'Goodness!' said Davie. 'This is a very serious departure. Will you be able to cope with the emergency?'

Mrs Goode laughed at that—which enabled Davie to pass easily to his important question.

'What was that I heard, Mrs Goode, about someone getting into your wardrobe on that night? Was it true?'

Mrs Goode laid the cloak down on a chair and turned aside to pick up another shirt. He guessed that his question was not welcome.

'I'm sorry now I ever mentioned the matter,' said Mrs Goode. 'But it's hard to disbelieve your eyes when you know as much as I do about this room. I always keep the clothes in the same places. That evening I left those *commedia* clothes in their usual order—that is, Pantaloon nearest to me, then the Doctor, then Columbine—the others, of course, were all in the dressing-rooms—and next day the Doctor's clothes were hanging nearest to me. I didn't see how I could be wrong about that. Someone had moved it. Must have done.'

'And yet there had been no break-in, no loss of anything?'

'No. Nothing.'

'You mean that you left them as they are now, and you found them—may I?' said Davie, moving the Pantaloon costume from the first to the second station—'like this? The Doctor's costume nearest to you?'

'Yes,' said Mrs Goode.

'That's very odd, certainly,' said Davie, moving the Doctor's clothes to their proper number two position.

'It was. But that's four months ago—and, as I say, I'm sorry now that I mentioned it. No one ever made any sense of it, and sometimes I wonder, after all, if I did imagine it. It's never got any clearer for thinking about it.'

There was one more question that Davie needed to ask. 'How is your grand-daughter doing?'

'Very well, thank you.'

'I saw her on that occasion.'

'Ah,' said Mrs Goode, 'I was wondering how you could have known about her. Well, now she's got herself engaged to be married.'

'I hope that's a good idea.'

'I hope so,' said Mrs Goode, making a wry sort of face. 'He's an actor, unfortunately. At another acting school—Renton's. I was against it for a long time. But opposition only exposed her to something worse. You see we're back to Alan Bastable. He was after her, and I wasn't going to have that. When he'd gone I was sorry I'd ever interfered over Ian Rammage. He's a brute, too. They're all brutes, dear. But at least he's not married. So I suppose it's for the best.'

'I hope so, Mrs Goode. Well, I must go and find myself some dinner. After which—'

' "Farewell glorious villains",' said Mrs Goode unexpectedly.

'Precisely. I'm looking forward to it. Goodbye.'

'Goodbye, dear.'

For a full half minute after Davie had gone, Mrs Goode, iron in hand, stood gazing at the closed door. She had been letting her tongue run away. She knew that. She didn't see that it mattered, but she wondered how she had been so easily persuaded to talk, and why her visitor had been so interested, after all this time, in Alan Bastable. And what was the point in his fiddling about with the hangers? It wasn't a matter that positively demanded demonstration.

But Davie, walking down the drive, was telling himself exactly the opposite. Demonstration had been the purpose of his visit. She saw me do it, he was thinking, and yet she didn't understand what I did. She thought she did, but she was wrong. It's not conclusive—of course it's not. But it shows there are two ways of looking at it. One way makes possible sense, the other doesn't. It surely isn't unreasonable to prefer the way that makes sense.

At the gate he halted a moment, fished out his notebook, and wrote down 'Florence Bastable'. Then he set off towards the Green Dragon. And as he went along Merton Road he told himself that he had been singularly fortunate. He had found three things in Mrs Goode's wardrobe: one conviction and two names.

The names were Florence Bastable and Ian Rammage. He would have to confirm it when he got back (luckily he had kept the programme) but he felt sure that Ian Rammage, the brute who had claimed Laura for his own, was the young man who had been Pantaloon on Saturday night, the young man he had seen reflected in the dressing-room looking-glass, the young man with the large red ring, the young man who had seen only the first part of the show on that night in November.

The conviction was a different kind of knowledge. It concerned the *commedia* costumes. He was sure now that no one had ever moved the Doctor's costume from its station on the rack. That was the thing that hadn't made sense. Either the tale was false, invented by Mrs Goode for some private reason of necessity, or Mrs Goode had misread the meaning of her own discovery.

Now Dr Davie was always influenced by his emotions. He liked Mrs Goode. And he made his choice accordingly.

IX

Dinner at the Green Dragon was precisely the same dinner as that of the previous November. It was all right. It was food of a sort. Nothing out of a tin bears the smallest resemblance to its original, but it can be agreeable in its own strange way. Davie mopped up the fruit salad and returned to the theatre.

The foyer was crowded. It was the last week of term, a first night, and the first night of an unusual play. The local supporters had turned out in force. Major Parkin, Mrs Torriano, Miss Mannering, Mrs Pheasant and Ruby: they were all there, and close by the box office was Miss Pringle. Two hours earlier that would have been an embarrassment. Now it was fortunate.

'You've come to see us again, Dr Davie. That *is* nice,' said Miss Pringle.

'I haven't got a ticket,' said Davie. 'I hope there's room.'

'We'll find somewhere,' said Miss Pringle. 'We *are* rather full tonight, I know. There's a party from a school, and I do hope they know what they're coming to. They did *Lysistrata* here once, and there was a dreadful misunderstanding about one of the matinées. It was Christmas time and the head mistress of a primary school thought it was a pantomime.'

'*Lysistrata and the Seven Dwarfs*' said Davie.

'Yes. Now, I tell you what I can do, Dr Davie. Mr Pomeroy's away. You can sit in his box.'

'Would that be permissible?'

'Oh yes. Mr Pomeroy doesn't mind a bit. If you'll come with me I'll let you in.'

'I must know what happened at the *Lysistrata* matinée,' said Davie.

'They sat it out. I think the head mistress was enjoying it, and the children didn't understand. So it was all right in the end. This way. It will be much nicer for you in the box.'

In a far corner of the foyer Tito Adriano was standing with Harriet Bastable. It was five months since either of them had visited the Winston Theatre. Harriet pulled Tito's sleeve.

'Who's that?' said Harriet.

'Where?'

'There, with Priscilla.'

'It's an old chap who's interested in the *commedia*—called Davie. He was at the show the other night. He said he'd been at the performance here in November.'

'It's not *commedia* tonight,' said Harriet.

'I suppose he wants to see *The White Devil*. It's not often done.'

Harriet considered. 'He was twice at the school *after* it happened,' she said. 'Talking to Edward. I saw him.'

'They wanted everyone's evidence.'

'They wanted it once. He didn't have to come back.'

'Well?'

'I was wondering—'

'Come on.'

'I was wondering,' said Harriet, lowering her voice, 'if he's as interested in the theatre as he pretends to be. You were doing the same show at Renton's. Why did he want to see it again? Why's he here now?'

Tito raised one eyebrow. He said nothing. Harriet was an absurd woman. For Tito it was one of her charms.

'Well, would *you* keep coming out to this slaughter-house

of the drama just for the sake of the play?' Harriet demanded. 'I wouldn't.'

'I don't see that it matters,' said Tito, leading Harriet to the bar. 'What do you want? The usual?'

Miss Pringle led Davie to Mr Pomeroy's box. 'Here we are,' she said. 'I hope you'll enjoy it.'

'Thanks very much,' said Davie. 'I am honoured.'

He shut the door and looked about him. 'Not comfortable enough for visitors,' Mr Pomeroy had said. The box was small, but it had two seats, and was perfectly comfortable. He just didn't want any more of my company, said Davie to himself. It's a point of view I have encountered before.

He settled himself down, glanced through the programme and then had a look round the theatre. It was entertaining to command a secret view of the entire audience. On that night in November he had been sitting in the second row, but from here Mr Pomeroy must have seen everything and everybody. Provided he'd stayed to the end. Perhaps he hadn't stayed till the end. He could have slipped in and out as he pleased and no one the wiser. On that morning after the tragedy, when Davie had seen him in his office, looking so utterly worn out, naturally he hadn't questioned him about his movements. It would have been impossible. It wasn't his business, and he hadn't even thought about it. But, thinking about it now—why, yes, Mr Pomeroy might not have been in here at all. There are so many unknowns, thought Davie, so many shaky assumptions, in this business.

And then the subject was changed for him by voices immediately beneath the ledge of the box.

'Is *The White Devil* about the colour bar?' asked Ruby Pheasant.

'Oh no, dear,' said Miss Mannering. 'I don't think so. It was written some time ago. It will be about love, and revenge, and murder, I expect. It always is if it's a tragedy. A comedy is only about love—and everyone has to be very amusing all the time. I think I like revenge better. It's nearer to life than all those witty lines are. People don't think as fast as that: but they're always ready for a fight.'

And that's basic dramatic criticism, thought Davie, as the auditorium lights began to fade.

A moment later he was looking at a street in Rome, dimly lit and sinister. And then the play began with that lone whip-crack of a word—'Banish'd'.

All those poisonings and assassinations! Crude, some might call it. Not Davie. The previous summer, in Italy, he had driven past Bracciano and seen the great Orsini castle on the hill above the town. It had belonged to this same Duke, the Bracciano of the play: and, from those battlements, his mistress, Vittoria Accoramboni, "the White Devil", must have looked down upon the tranquil lake. Perhaps the poisons and the flashing swords were not employed as often as the Jacobean dramatists chose to think. But they were real people, the people of this play, dangerous people, and that is how they sound in Webster's language—real and dangerous. Davie was enchanted.

When the interval came Miss Pringle lured him out to give him a cup of coffee. Grateful for the courtesy, he regretted the interruption. The gossip of North London sounded silly after Vittoria's dazzling answers in the trial scene. She was all that they said she was—whore and acquainted with murder—but it was impossible not to be her partisan. Davie detested that vile cardinal.

'May I introduce you to Mr Wynter?' said Miss Pringle. 'Mr Wynter's our bursar.'

Davie said 'How d'you do', and for a moment both of them seemed tongue-tied. Wynter was awkward with strangers: but Davie was calling to mind how he had seen Derek Wynter framed in the doorway of his office, a man dismayed, and later that same November night, after the play, his face dramatically lighted by a lamp outside a door. Those were different faces from the one he wore now. Derek Wynter seemed a pleasant easy-going young man. There was nothing dramatic about him.

Davie said, 'I wonder if either of you can tell me who started this extraordinary idea that a girl's eyes are somehow promoted by putting white lines round them? At any distance a white line looks like a white line.'

'Is it supposed to be a high light?' asked Miss Pringle.

'A high light round the eyes creates an impression of exophthalmic goitre,' said Davie. 'I don't think they know that.'

Derek Wynter laughed. 'You're absolutely right,' he said. 'And they don't know. Women will do anything to their eyes, anything. The idea is not to be attractive, but to be noticed. At least, so one supposes.'

'It was Isabella who looked so ghastly,' said Davie. 'No wonder her husband had her murdered.'

'It's time you went back to your seats,' said Miss Pringle. 'I shall pass on your comments about white lines.'

As Davie and Wynter walked back to the theatre Davie said, 'We've never met, but I remember seeing you last November. I was at that *commedia dell'arte* show.'

Derek Wynter said, 'Were you?' He did not go on. Plainly he was not accepting Davie's cue. And for that moment he looked again like the man Davie had seen in the bursary. Then 'I have to use this door for my seat,' he said. 'Goodbye. It was nice seeing you.'

He hasn't come into this story—so far as I know, thought Davie, as he waited in his box for the auditorium lights to fade. He'd certainly been having words with Alan Bastable that day, which might be interesting if only one knew what words they were. Which one never will.

In the second part of *The White Devil* the play grows strangely twisted. The Duchess has been poisoned, Vittoria's husband strangled. Blood breeds blood. Revenge must be satisfied. Marcello, Ludovico, Bracciano, Zanche—all must die. Vittoria must die. Flamineo must die. The play must end in black disaster. "Farewell, glorious villains!" the lost Flamineo calls to his dead friends. Strangest apostrophe! There are no nerves in this dreadful story.

Slowly the lights went down upon the tragedy and rose upon that homely audience. And immediately, incongruous and too soon, he found Miss Pringle by his side, gaily eager to enquire how Dr Davie had enjoyed himself.

'Very much,' said Davie. 'I came down to see Martin Searle. I think he was good.'

'Oh, you must tell him so! Would you like to come behind?'

'Well—no—I wouldn't,' said Davie. 'I'm not very good at making complimentary visits. One runs out of subjects so soon. But I'd like to send him a note. Would you be very kind and give it to him?'

'With pleasure.'

Davie had come provided. He fished out of his pocket a piece of paper and an envelope.

On the paper he wrote,

> Dear Martin—It's late. This is to tell you I did enjoy the play, and I think you were very good. But it would be better to talk than write about it. Will you come to dinner with me at the Chesterfield Club on Tuesday—tomorrow? That's a day you don't perform. Please ring up. Leave a message with the porter if I'm not there. Seven-thirty.
>
> Yours
> R. V. Davie

He put the letter in the envelope, stuck it down and addressed it. Then, 'Thank you very much,' said Davie, handing the letter to Miss Pringle, 'and thank you for your kindness in arranging this lordly box for my pleasure.'

'Not at all,' said Miss Pringle. 'It was lovely to see you here again. Good night.'

'Good night.'

And so Davie made his way out of the theatre and joined the last of the audience as they walked down the drive.

'I don't think it was a very nice play,' Ruby Pheasant was saying as he passed by. 'There wasn't anyone except the old mother who was what you'd call nice, was there?'

'No, dear,' said Miss Mannering. 'There wasn't. And *she* wasn't right in the head.'

'I'm glad we don't live in those old times,' said Mrs Pheasant. 'With all those evil passions.'

Davie reached the school gates and stepped into the lamplight. Ahead were the lights of the Green Dragon, and, across the road, the light by the bus stop. It all seemed civilized and bright. Far, far away, according to Mrs Pheasant, was all that dark Renaissance wickedness, the evil passions of the bad old days. But, as he walked down Merton Road, Davie was thinking, not of Flamineo with a sword in his guts, but of Alan Bastable with a knife in his back—he, too, "i'th' way to study a long silence".

x

When he got back to the Chesterfield it was eleven o'clock. He went straight up to his room. Since Saturday night a strange story had been growing in his mind. This afternoon it had been, not exactly confirmed, but strengthened by something Mrs Goode had failed to say. This evening it had been, not exactly confirmed, but strengthened by reflections upon Mr Pomeroy and Mr Wynter.

On that night in November Davie had seen Martin Searle in his seat at the beginning of the show. He had not noticed that he had not returned to it after the interval. How many other things had he not noticed? Who could say where Mr Pomeroy was during the second play? In the box all the time? Or not? Who could say where Derek Wynter was? Davie had not seen either of them. There was no evidence behind these reflections. It was only that—well, they fitted in with other reflections. For instance, they fitted in with what Mrs Goode had failed to say.

It was all very puzzling, thought Davie as he emptied his pockets and laid everything on the dressing-table according to an established ritual.

His money he built up into a glittering pagoda, tapering from a base of silver pieces of fifty to a roof of new pennies.

As he did this he was telling himself that he would put the whole thing out of his head until the next day. If it were a bright morning, he would take an early walk. If it were not, then an early bus, a bus going east towards the city.

He finished the pagoda, sat down and took his shoes off. The damned things were much more difficult to reach than they used to be. Then he got up, took his suit off and hung it reverently in the wardrobe. That was something he never failed to do. And, yes, he thought, there was just a chance he might find something interesting down there. Not anything the police did not know: obviously not: but conceivably something they had not appreciated.

And that being decided, he put the Bastable case sharply out of mind, tossed his flimsier clothes unceremoniously upon a chair, skipped into bed, put on his spectacles and reached for *A Cloistered Death*. He wouldn't be easy till he knew who had killed Canon Prettyman during the organ recital.

Oddly enough it was the organist. He had conveyed a powerful tape recording of a Bach fugue into the organ loft, thus providing himself with what should have been an equally powerful alibi. And would have been so but for the sagacity of old Miss Meakin (the local detective) who happened to be sitting at the back of the nave and was greatly puzzled by an execution immensely superior to the organist's usual performance.

'I suppose that's all right,' said Davie a little dubiously. He snipped out the light. Obviously the fool organist ought to have recorded himself.

For a few minutes he lay in the darkness, reflecting on the frangibility of alibis. Then 'You'd make a lovely Doctor, dear, with your legs', he whispered. He had been fascinated by that phrase from the beginning.

XI

It proved a lovely morning. At nine o'clock he left the Chesterfield, walked through a silent Shepherd Market, and so proceeded along Piccadilly down the Haymarket, towards Charing Cross.

By the National Gallery he paused for a minute to look down on the fountains of Trafalgar Square. He could never understand how people could gawp admiringly at the vulgar absurdities of the Trevi in Rome. Big fountains should be dignified, as these were.

The huge square was almost empty. In their accustomed south-east corner a mass of stupid pigeons stood sulkily waiting for their admirers to arrive, scattering breakfast.

Davie walked on past St Martin in the Fields and turned left into the Strand, which owes its name to the fact that it was once the next thing to the water. Bits of England are always tumbling into the sea. Sometimes we win a little back: the tidal waters of the Thames were taught their places long ago.

Davie had glorious memories of the Strand (alas, for Romano's and the Gaiety!) and though so much of it was gone, he still delighted in the street and its surrounding mysteries.

There is everything here from foreign stamps, slide rules and clothes, (men's clothes exclusively) to hotels, theatres, banks, and government offices, all competing to entice the passer-by to sunny New South Wales, exciting Queensland or beautiful Western Australia. To the right, side streets dip down towards the river, to the left slope upwards to the publishers, to David

Garrick's house, to all the carrots and lettuces and oranges of
Covent Garden, to the Opera House and Drury Lane.

At the end of the street you look left to the great portico of
Irving's Lyceum Theatre, right to Waterloo Bridge and ahead to
Wren's lovely church of St Mary Le Strand, overshadowed by,
but gloriously aloof from, the vast pomposity of Bush House.

And there on the right, harmonious with the little church, is
the great palace of Somerset House, the site once of magnificent
living, but now accommodating the documents of mortality.
They knew all about you, the people who work within those
walls—who was born where, who married whom, and who died
when, and what they left behind them. And most important, they
knew who benefited, besides the Treasury, from all this living
and dying.

It was to this repository of the truth that Davie was making
his early pilgrimage.

It is all very easy if you know the date, and only a little
harder if you don't. Records of Births to the left, records of
Marriages and Deaths to the right: the three great events of life
reduced to a line each in three indexes. Davie went to the room
on the left, looked up the date of Alan Bastable's birth, made an
application and paid his fee. Then he walked across the hall and
looked in the marriage registers and made another application.
The day was Tuesday. On Thursday at noon the certificates
would be waiting for him.

Then he walked across the great court. To right and left the
doorways are marked Inland Revenue. They know all about your
income here too. Somerset House has you completely docketed.

On the far side of the court a door leads to the hall containing
the indexes of wills. You no longer pay your shilling for the
right to search—it is free. If you know what you want you don't
have to wait. An attendant brings you the will at once. If you
want a copy, that takes time and costs ten pence for each separate
sheet: but if you only want to read it—to make such notes as
you can carry in your head, or discreetly on the back of an

envelope—you can find all you want to know immediately. Davie wanted to know the terms of the last will and testament of Miss Florence Bastable: and he had it before him fifteen minutes later.

It was briefly stated. "I leave everything of which I die possessed to Alan Bastable of ... and request that he will always retain the ring given me by his father".

Davie closed the ledger and returned it to its custodian. Then he crossed the great court again and re-entered the Strand. And presently he boarded a No. 15 bus. It would take him much of his way back to the Chesterfield.

There were only two other men on the top deck. They were at the back. Davie walked forward to the front seat. It was pleasant to look down on London on a spring morning. Earth had not anything to show that he loved better.

"And request that he will always retain the ring given me by his father." Davie repeated the words secretly to himself. They did not advance his enquiries. But they illuminated the picture of Alan Bastable. The young man had fulfilled his trust in life. But where now was his inheritance?

As the bus swept past Nelson's Column Davie noted that there were many more people in the square. The pigeons were ravenously devouring elevenses from the hand of infatuated visitors. And other visitors were devotedly photographing their friends feeding the pigeons. It would be non-stop eating now till nightfall.

Davie got off at Piccadilly Circus, and walked home through Mayfair, a delightful district where the eighteenth and twentieth centuries meet, illuminated by plane trees. Part of the time he was thinking how much he loved it all, and part of the time he was thinking about Miss Bastable and her ring. *The* ring. Each small discovery urged him on towards something else. He was reminded now of a certain open invitation. I don't suppose it was really intended, thought Davie. All the same, I think I'll accept it.

'A telephone message for you, sir,' said Alfred as he entered the club. 'A gentleman called Searle will be pleased to have dinner tonight.'

'Thank you. That's just what I want to know. And will you very kindly get me a number. This is it. Which box shall I use?'

'Number Three, if you please,' said Alfred.

XII

Tito Adriano was painting Harriet's portrait when the telephone rang—or rather he was at that early stage of sketching a foundation design on a canvas.

Tito was never idle. The term was over at Renton's. He had no other engagements. This was the time to paint Harriet in all her glory.

She sat by the window dressed in elaborate black, a black mantilla raised over a high comb. Only her garnets brought a flash of colour at her ears and neck and fingers.

'Let it go,' said Harriet.

But Tito did not like unanswered calls. It might be an invitation to work at Covent Garden, Glyndebourne, Drury Lane, even New York. Always Tito was the grand optimist. He went to the telephone.

'Yes? Oh yes. Certainly, I do. Not at all. No—I would be very happy. Please do. Tomorrow morning? It would be quite convenient. About noon? You know how to get here? Ah, yes, of course. Thank you.'

'And who was that?' asked Harriet.

'The old gentleman you were asking about last night, Dr Davie.'

Harriet was triumphant.

'What did I tell you?'

'I forget,' said Tito, fixing his attention on the canvas. 'What did you tell me?'

'I say that man wants something. Why is he always poking around?'

'He only wants to see my *commedia* pictures.'

'Your pictures!'

'What worries you? It was I who asked him to come.'

'I don't like nosy people.'

'Boo to that,' said Tito. 'I invited him. And stop bouncing about.'

'I shall be out.'

'Very well,' said Tito. 'I make a note. Harriet will be out. He will be greatly relieved. He wishes to see my pictures. Not you. Now keep still, or I won't paint you.'

Harriet kept still. She was most anxious that her elegance should be recorded.

And Davie left the telephone box, and made his way to the writing room. Not, of course, that he wanted to write. But he did not want to talk, and if you went into the morning-room you were certainly going to do that. It was a quarter past eleven, and he was exhausted. A long walk, three-quarters of an hour standing up at Somerset House, another walk, a carefully poised telephone call—truly, he had done a great deal that morning.

He settled down with *The Times* and was presently so uninterested in the world's distresses that he drifted off into a delicious doze, from which he awoke when the club began to fill up at about twelve.

'One of the imponderables in the area under discussion,' Adrian Ballsover was saying. So Davie got up and wandered into the bar. It was a little early, but he meant to lunch early. With Martin Searle coming to dinner he thought he needed a nice long lie-down in the afternoon. And then perhaps a walk round the block after tea.

'I would like a tonic water, please, and a slice of lemon,' Davie said to William the barman. 'And some gin,' he added after a moment's reflection.

XIII

'I have just had a great surprise,' said Davie, returning from a six o'clock stroll, to George Canteloupe. 'I passed a very charming young woman wearing not just a long dress but a Kate Greenaway dress down to the ankles. With a frill round the end of it, and a waist as high as nature allows. You remember how three years ago we were assured that never ever—'

'I do indeed.'

'Do you think this reaction will spread? I never could endure those knees. Fat or knobbly, they are all so distressingly well-pleased with themselves. I wonder—is there any hope for the crinoline or the bustle?'

'Not the crinoline, R. V. They'd never get into a taxi. And the underground at rush hours—'

'Yes, I suppose the crinoline is out. But I see no reason why they shouldn't return to the bustle. Now *that* was an entertaining, thought-provoking way of advertising a popular feature. It might go very well in the present age.'

'For one of your enormous antiquity, R. V.—'

'I thank you.'

'You are commendably pre-occupied with the present.'

'If that is a delicate way of saying that I ought to be thinking about Death,' said Davie, 'I must tell you that I don't. Though I do sometimes wonder if he's thinking about me.'

George Canteloupe looked at his watch. 'It is twenty past seven,' he said, and the words seemed to bear a meaning deeper than a mere statement of fact. And so Davie understood it. 'Not tonight, George,' he said. 'I am expecting a guest. An ornament of the dazzling present. It will be interesting to see how *he* will be dressed.'

Martin Searle was dressed most becomingly. Vain, as Davie was vain, he enjoyed his clothes and spent too much money on them. His trousers were wide at the ends, close at the knees, and in the more northerly parts fitted him like a skin. He wore a white shirt with a sapphire blue tie and a deep blue velvet jacket. His long hair had recently been tempered by the hand of fashion. It was short compared with the hair of two years ago. It was tidy. Sitting down he looked like someone in a Jane Austen novel. Standing up he looked like the present. That was the trousers.

Davie was fascinated by those trousers, and wondered if he dare get a pair himself. The trouble was of course that Carnaby Street and King's Road measurements go no higher than 36 round the middle, and he was—well, certainly 37. And he hardly thought he could ask Mr Thankful to make him a pair. Mr Thankful would blench at such familiarities.

Davie had reserved a table in the corner of the dining-room. He had chosen a respectable wine. And the Chesterfield dinner was not at all bad. There was a particularly delectable fruit called an ugli which turns up at curiously irregular intervals. There was a best end of neck—presumably a great number of best ends of neck. There was some very early asparagus. Expensive, but what's the use of money if you don't spend it, said Davie to his conscience the moment it started raising its eyebrows. What nonsense! Asparagus certainly.

Martin began by asking Davie how he had got on at Renton's, and, that being soon answered, they came naturally to *The White Devil* and to Martin's performance in it. It was the right order.

Davie had seen the play fifty years before, when women's parts at Cambridge were still taken by men. There was that to talk about. 'I can never think why it should be assumed that Shakespeare's heroines were necessarily taken by fourteen-year-old boys. I've seen Clytemnestra, Electra, Cressida, Vittoria, and lots of other parts taken by men in their twenties—with absolute conviction.'

'And there's the National Theatre Rosalind and Celia,' said Martin.

And that led to Flamineo. It was not difficult for Davie to praise Martin's performance. He had enjoyed it. 'You'll be damned lucky,' he said, 'if you ever get a part as good as that in the professional theatre. You can't all be blazing stars. Enjoy yourself while you can.'

Martin, not less than other actors, was happy to be praised, but he did not hold Davie down to the subject. He was a sensitive young man, and it was he who presently changed the subject. He and Davie had just pondered whether they would have treacle tart or cold apple pie (the staple dishes of all right-minded clubs) when Martin said, 'I thought, when we met the other day, that you were still interested in that Bastable affair. Have you considered any more about it?'

'Yes, I have,' said Davie.

'I thought you might have done,' said Martin.

Davie was a little taken aback. He had expected to do a good deal of manoeuvring before introducing that subject again.

'There are some things I'd like to talk over with you,' he said.

Martin paused a moment. Then, 'Are you anything to do with the police?' he asked. 'Because, if you are, I think you ought to say so.'

'No, no,' said Davie. 'I'm only an inquisitive old fool who gets fascinated by apparently insoluble puzzles. There *is* a solution to everything. And I don't like being defeated. The alleged, the accepted, facts in this story are provoking. I think we want some new ones. That's what's been interesting me.'

'Have you got some new ones?'

'Not facts exactly—but new interpretations of facts, yes, I think so. But we'll have to move before I tell you about them. Now, if you'll wait outside a moment while I pay my bill, we'll have some coffee. And then I'll take you up to the library. It's certain to be empty at this time of day.'

So Davie approached the cash desk and exchanged compliments with Miss Mittens, its genteel custodian; and Martin stood outside the door and looked at a ticker-tape hysterically reporting items of no interest in a little glass dome; and at least three members of the club took a long look at Martin looking at the ticker-tape. It was not often that the Chesterfield saw anything so ornamentally suitable within its eighteenth century walls.

Ten minutes later the two were sitting by the library window. As Davie had anticipated, the room was empty. There are scholars at the Chesterfield: but they are not so abandoned as to use the library after dinner.

'I didn't *have* to exercise my mind on this problem,' said Davie. 'Nobody asked me to help. Nor were my loyalties or affections involved. But I couldn't stop thinking about it. The reason was quite simple. I could not accept the idea that Bastable was stabbed in the wings while waiting to take his call. It looked like that. But I could not, and I do not, see that there was time. When I went to the show at Renton's I took a stop-watch with me. It recorded that eighty seconds was the outside time that anyone could have had to commit a murder, hide the body, and escape. I don't believe it was possible.'

'It does seem a bit steep, I agree,' said Martin.

'My second decision was to reject, because of intrinsic improbability, the idea that he was killed elsewhere, after the show, and subsequently put where he was found. Again, it's too difficult. Too many people about.'

'Of course.'

'And there would have been blood somewhere else.. There wasn't. But if I reject both those possibilities, I am in a jam. I have to suggest something else.'

'And that something else,' said Martin, 'is going to be something more difficult than either of the other two. What you're suggesting is that Alan was killed during the show.'

Davie looked a little embarrassed. 'That's what I've tried to tell myself, yes.'

'You're saying that Alan was dead when he was wheeled off by Clown?'

'I thought it might be possible.'

'But, Dr Davie, what about Clown's evidence that Alan got off the barrow as soon as they got into the wings?'

'I know. But one has to consider everything and everybody without any kind of indulgence. Suppose Clown were an accomplice. Suppose Tito were an accomplice. What if Tito went to the O.P. side for the precise reason of confirming Clown's evidence? If Clown and Tito and someone else on stage were in collaboration, it could have been a team job. It's difficult, but it's possible.'

'I'd say impossible,' said Martin. 'I'm thinking of the stage. I don't believe this. And from the—well, careful way you talk, I don't think that you do either.'

'One has to think these things out in order to reject them. You can't destroy ideas without first building them up and looking at them. I did think it was possible. But then I decided that this also was too difficult. I'm glad to have your swift confirmation of that. Thinking's never wasted. If one's wrong one knows one has to think of something else.'

'And did you?'

'Yes, I did. And this is where I particularly want your opinion. I have built up a strange theory. Not at all on guess-work. You can tell me if I make sense.'

'I'll try.'

'All along I've been troubled by two things. First, when Bastable was found he was not wearing his mask. I can see no reason why it should have fallen off. And, at first sight, there seems no reason why the murderer should have taken it off. Why then was it lying on the ground?'

'You think that's important?'

'I think it's the heart of the matter. The second mystery concerns Alan Bastable's ring. He was wearing it during the play. It was you who told me that he wasn't wearing it when he was found. Why wasn't he wearing it? Is it conceivable that, with only seconds to spare, a murderer would bother to take off a ring?'

'Only if the ring were valuable and the reason for the murder.'

'But that's just what I distrust. If theft were the motive, the ring could have been stolen in some easier way. Caught in the act, a thief commits murder. But he doesn't commit murder purely as a step towards committing a theft.'

Martin Searle considered. 'He was wearing it during the play. He was not wearing it when he was found. Aren't you back to the idea you've already rejected—that he was killed after he came off? How else could it have disappeared?'

'Oh, yes,' said Davie. 'That's the logic of it. But I don't believe it.'

Martin Searle stirred in his seat. He felt the argument was deteriorating. 'You don't believe he was killed during the applause. You don't believe he was killed after the show was over. You don't believe he was killed on the stage. You must believe something,' he said.

Davie waited for a few seconds before replying. Then, 'Do you remember that cock and bull story you told me about Mrs Goode complaining that someone had moved the Doctor's costume in the wardrobe?'

'Yes.'

'I had got a flutter of an idea about this mask and ring mystery, and at first I tried to fit it in with the Doctor's costume. Could there have been an X, a third masked character, disguised as the Doctor, wearing a costume borrowed from the wardrobe, a costume significantly returned to the wrong place on the rack? It seemed an attractive dramatic idea. But it led nowhere. I could not see this person. He wasn't there. But then I thought of something important and very simple. If there are two things hanging on a rack, you get the same result if you move A behind B or B in front of A. It occurred to me that because Mrs Goode saw the Doctor's costume nearest to her she assumed that it had been moved forward. But what if it were the Pantaloon costume that had been taken away, and afterwards returned by mistake to a position behind the Doctor's? I moved the Pantaloon clothes before her eyes. She still thought I'd moved the Doctor's. That was what she was expecting me to do. She didn't seem to take in what I'd really done.'

'How do you know? Mrs Goode doesn't miss much.'

'You are right to be exact. No, I don't know. But I believe she did not understand. Now, suppose someone with a key had entered the wardrobe. Suppose he had dressed himself in Pantaloon's clothes?'

Martin Searle stared at Davie. This was something new.

'Two *Pantaloons*?'

'He could have killed Bastable *before* Pantaloon's entry in the second play—when everyone else was already on stage. He could have killed him then, hidden him, and then played Pantaloon's part—'

'*He, the murderer?*'

'Why not? It's all mime. He could have played his part, and escaped quite easily to the wardrobe long before the applause was over. He'd have been in his ordinary clothes in sixty seconds and away down the drive before the audience was out and away.

'Now, obviously, he'd have had to take Bastable's mask in order to play the part, and if he wanted to be perfect, he'd have had to take his ring too. When he came off at the end there would have been no time to restore these things properly—but obviously it was essential that the mask should be left behind. So he had to drop it near the body. That's fair, isn't it?'

'Yes.'

'On the other hand, it would not have made sense to drop the ring. And it would have been difficult to return it to Bastable's hand. He couldn't drop it. He had to take it. Possibly he might not even have remembered that he was wearing it. But however you look at it, the ring goes, the mask stays. How does that strike you?'

'It's tremendously ingenious, Dr Davie—it's absolutely super—'

' "But" is the word you are feeling for,' said Davie.

'Yes,' said Searle with an apologetic smile. 'But it offers no evidence.'

'Absolutely none.'

'It doesn't advance the search. That could be the way it was done. But the question is still, who did it?'

'After all this time there *is* no evidence—except this ring. What would *you* do if you had committed a murder and carried the evidence on your finger? Drop it over the side in mid-channel? Lose it on the middle of Dartmoor? Or would you be mad enough to keep it and give it to the girl friend? Or keep it, and wear it on the stage? Or keep it just for possession's sake?'

'I'd drop it in the sea.'

'Even if it were valuable?'

'Yes.'

'Very valuable? Something like the Koh-i-noor?'

'No, I suppose I wouldn't.'

'Greed usually wins. If this ring is of no value,' said Davie, 'I reckon no one will ever find out who murdered Alan Bastable. But if it *is* valuable, I'm not so sure. Certainly the murderer took the ring . . . You are not impressed by my theory?'

'Yes, I am. Very impressed. But it isn't the Koh-i-noor we're talking about. It's just Alan's garnet ring.'

'That's very true. You sober me down, Martin.'

For several seconds Martin Searle sat still, fixing his eyes on the bookcases beyond Davie's head. Then he said, 'I suppose you realize that your theory cuts out any of the actors in the play; cuts out Peter; cuts out Tito. No one inside the show could have done it.'

'No.'

'But it also means—'

'Exactly,' said Davie. 'You are with me.'

'It also means it could only be done by someone who knew the stage business.'

'Such as—'

'Anyone who'd rehearsed the part with Tito before. There are several who have. And not only at this school. Or anyone who'd watched a lot of rehearsals.'

'Such as—'

'Derek Wynter.'

'Who's he?'

'The bursar.'

'Yes, of course.'

'He's often in the theatre. Or Edward Pomeroy. Or Mrs Goode. She knows it all backwards. Quite a lot of people do.'

'Indeed?' said Davie. 'Just now you were cutting me down to size. Now you are leading me on.'

'I'm only answering your questions,' said Martin.

'Answer me another. Who could reliably identify Alan Bastable's ring?'

'Harriet, I suppose.'

'Of course. But obviously, if she knew where it was, she would have identified it already.'

'Michael Teed.'

'He dressed with Bastable?'

'Yes. During that show he did.'

'In two days I suspect he may not have considered it very closely.'

'Laura. She must have seen it.'

'Indeed yes. I actually saw her put it on her finger.'

'You did?'

'But I would not rely on her accuracy. Anyone else?'

Martin thought for a few seconds. Then he said, 'Priscilla. Priscilla Pringle. She's in contact with everyone. And she was friendly with Alan. I'm sure she would have seen it. It's quite likely Alan showed it to her. He wouldn't show it to anyone else—but he would have shown it to her.'

'That's interesting,' said Davie, and fell into a long silence.

Presently Martin said, 'Thank you for dinner. I think I ought to be going now.'

'Ah,' said Davie, as though returning to the conversation from a long distance. 'Keep all this to yourself, won't you? I've been saying a lot of strange things. Don't repeat them.'

'I won't. But may I ask if you're going to the police with this theory?'

'I don't see how I can. What's it based on except my conjectures? They wouldn't welcome a beautifully tailored theory without a single fact to support it.'

'Mrs Goode's costumes?'

'That's not a fact. She admitted rather grudgingly that she might have imagined it.'

'But, even so, someone might have borrowed the Pantaloon clothes.'

'Someone might have done so. But that's still not a fact. My theory is as much balanced on a cloud as any theory ever was.'

Davie said good-night at the club door, and stood there for a few seconds watching Martin till he turned the corner. I don't really see why I shouldn't get a pair of trousers like that, he said to himself.

Back in the writing-room he returned to his speculations. As much balanced on a cloud as any theory ever was, he repeated. But it's rather a nice theory all the same. And talking about things irons them out.

Talking about things. He had certainly done that. But there had been one thing he had kept back. He had said nothing about Somerset House. He had felt an old-fashioned delicacy about that. He had not wanted to discuss Miss Bastable's will with Martin Searle. Besides, he might have sounded melo-dramatic, and that was something quite alien to Dr R. V. Davie.

For some minutes he sat there staring at the ornamental fender. In his heart he knew what he believed. But I can't prove it, thought Davie.

And there's nothing more I can do about it. Except one thing—and that's at a risk.

But after a few seconds' consideration he got up and walked

down the passage to the telephones. Of those four, Harriet, Laura, Miss Pringle, and Michael Teed, Miss Pringle was certainly the only one he could approach.

It was half-past ten. The show would be over and she was likely to be at home. He entered one of the telephone boxes and rang her up.

XIV

'I hope you have not come on a wild duck chase,' said Tito Adriano. 'You may have seen all my pictures before. I have picked out the Pantalone ones.' (He did not use the English variation, Pantaloon). 'I do not see any rings. For instance, here is a very clear picture of Stefanello Bottarga, who was a kind of Pantalone character. There he is with his great fingers outstretched—but not a ring.'

'No. But I also notice that nobody else wears a ring. Not even the ladies. It could be that the artist couldn't be bothered with small details.'

'Yes. They were poor players. Perhaps they hadn't got any jewellery.'

'Poor players delighted in jewellery in the straight theatre.'

'Yes,' said Tito, wagging an argumentative finger, 'but the straight theatre was different from a *commedia* show on a trestle stage run up in a corner of the fairground. Those actors may not have had any jewellery, and in any case I guess they were as superior to jewellery as a mime actor is superior to props.'

'I'm sure you're right there. Still, I've never met an actress who didn't love a necklace.'

'You look through the pictures, Dr Davie, and I'll make us a drink,' said Tito. 'What would you like?'

'You are very kind. It's early for a drink.'

'Oh no.'

'Then may I have a gin and tonic, please, and truly not much gin.'

Tito withdrew to the kitchen. Davie sifted through the prints. Many of them he knew already. Some were new. They were interesting. But (as Harriet had astutely suspected) Davie had not come to Amelia Gardens to look at prints. He had wanted to see more of Tito Adriano. He had wanted to find out if Tito had anything to add about Alan Bastable's ring. He was (Davie believed) in close touch with Harriet Bastable. If Harriet knew anything about the ring it was reasonable to suppose that Tito would know as much.

It was not difficult to bring the matter into the conversation. 'There are certainly no rings here,' said Davie after Tito had handed him his drink. 'I suppose wearing a ring was just Alan Bastable's whim, and the other chap at Renton's picked up the idea from him.'

'I expect so. I think perhaps Alan always wore that ring, and just did not take it off.'

'Were you familiar with it?'

'No, not at all. I was only at the school two days a week. One merely knew that he had a ring.'

'And no one ever found it?'

'No. His wife said it was valuable. But what could she do?'

'Was it insured?'

'No, it wasn't.'

'Then it hardly sounds as though it were valuable.'

'I agree.'

'I see you are a painter, too,' said Davie, pointing to the easel. 'May I look?'

'They go together. I produce. I design my own sets. And so I paint.'

At its present stage the picture might have been anyone. But although Tito had not yet brought the cold lights to her face, or the bright lights to her neck and ears, Davie guessed the sitter.

'It is—or it will be—Mrs Bastable,' said Tito, getting up and joining Davie by the canvas. 'I hope.'

'Is she Spanish?'

'She is English, but she had a Spanish grandfather. She likes to think she looks like one of the ladies in *Don Giovanni*. But her nature,' said Tito with a gentle smile, 'is more like one of the cats in *Carmen*.'

Davie raised his eyebrows.

'But she is extremely beautiful,' Tito added, as though earnest to correct a wrong impression.

'I must be going,' said Davie. 'It has been very kind of you to receive me and to let me see your pictures.'

'It has been a great pleasure,' said Tito.

And so Davie returned from Amelia Gardens, not thinking his visit had been productive of anything at all except to confirm that Tito was a cool and attractive person: and Tito went straight to his kitchen, not thinking of anything at all except that it was time to start making lunch.

First he sliced half an onion and delicately sautéd it in butter. Then he added the rice, and mingled rice, butter and onion in one glorious shining mass with the aid of a wooden spatula. Then he added a glass of white wine, and let it reduce to nothing.

Harriet, mounting the stairs, knew exactly what was cooking. Risotto à la Milanese. Good.

Tito was adding the first lot of chicken consommé as she entered the flat.

'What ho!' said Tito without turning round.

Harriet crossed the room and stood in the doorway.

'Well?' she asked. 'Was your learned visitor a success? What did you talk about?'

'Rings,' said Tito.

'Rings?'

'He wanted to know if any of the Pantalones in my pictures wore rings.'

'What for?'

'He just wanted to know if there was any tradition of wearing a ring.'

'And was there?'

'No.'

'Alan wore a ring.'

'So did Ian Rammage at Renton's. That's what made him ask.'

Tito added a second measure of consommé and gave the whole dish a stir with the spatula.

'Ian Rammage wore a ring, did he?' said Harriet.

'Yes.'

'Had he seen the Winston production?'

'Yes, he had. He was there that night as a matter of fact.'

Harriet moved back into the sitting-room. She never liked talking directly about last November.

'What else did you discuss with your distinguished visitor?'

'Your picture,' called Tito. 'He liked it.'

'Oh, did he?' said Harriet suddenly smiling as she crossed the room to inspect the picture. It seemed that her opinion of Dr Davie was suddenly mended. 'Even at this stage it's lovely, Tito. It really is. Do come and look.'

'I can't. This is a solemn moment,' said Tito, adding a final lot of consommé. He had steeped some saffron in that. 'This one is going to have hard-boiled egg, sultanas, and mushrooms. Will that do? I can't afford chicken or scampi today.'

Harriet returned to the doorway. 'You will be interested to hear that I saw your learned friend on my way back. And what do you think he was doing?'

'Tell me.'

'He was having a drink with Priscilla at the Green Dragon.'

'Was he?' said Tito. 'How remarkable.'

'It *is* remarkable, Tito. Why is he so interested in all of us?'

'The answer, my poor girl, is that he isn't. He's interested in me because of my work. He's interested in Priscilla because he's met her over school matters. But he hasn't shown the remotest interest in you, and I suppose that's what's galling you.'

'I could brain you, Tito,' said Harriet, 'if it wasn't for the fact that you haven't finished my picture.'

Tito quickly added some butter and grated cheese. 'Stop talking,' he said. 'The risotto is ready.'

XV

It was a little after one o'clock when Davie reached the Green Dragon. It was plainly the place for lunch. He entered the saloon bar, went to the counter, and ordered the same excellent meal that he had had before: cold beef and salad. He also asked for another gin and tonic. He did not want another gin and tonic, but there is a delicacy in these matters. You do not ask for a glass of water in a public house—though you would not be refused if you did.

Davie retired with his drink to the same small table in the corner where he had sat four months before, and it was only when he had sat himself down that he realized that Miss Pringle was at the neighbouring table. She was dealing with a glass of Guinness and some ham sandwiches.

'Hallo!' said Davie. 'Here I am again.'

Miss Pringle said, 'So you are,' and immediately blushed because it sounded silly. She had been surprised and unable to think of any remark suitable to the occasion. Here he was again—and what for this time, was naturally the enquiry which occupied her mind.

'I'm having a proper plate of cold English roast beef,' said Davie. 'A luxury, in my opinion. Ah, here it is. Thank you. I disapprove of Lord Sandwich's famous invention.'

'Bad for the figure?'

'For mine certainly.' Davie glanced round the bar. 'I don't see anyone from the school.'

'They don't come here much,' said Miss Pringle. 'We've a good canteen and a bar. And it's cheaper. So there's no point. They only come here if they feel like screaming and want to get away.'

'I hope you're not feeling like screaming?'

'Oh no, not a bit. But I like to get outside sometimes. Besides, the Dragon is fun. I like the pictures, don't you?'

'I do indeed—especially that one over there, with the fat man in the brook and the horse laughing at him on the other side of the hedge.'

Davie took up his glass, turned it about in his hand, took a sip, and put the glass back on the table. Miss Pringle took a bite off one of her sandwiches.

Presently Davie said, 'I didn't have a chance to ask you on Monday night. Do tell me. Did anyone ever find the explanation of that Bastable tragedy?'

Miss Pringle glanced quickly round the bar. There was no one there she knew, and no one particularly near.

'No,' she said. 'Never. I don't know what suspicions the police may have, or what evidence. But they've never acted, which must mean that they're not sure.'

'Or even less.'

'Or even less.'

'Who *was* Alan Bastable, Miss Pringle? I wish you'd tell me his background.'

Miss Pringle did not immediately answer.

'You're wondering why I want to know. I'll tell you. I've got a bee in my bonnet about this crime. I've ideas about it, which may be crazy, but at any rate they're different. I have decided that the clue to this mystery lies in Alan Bastable's ring—'

Miss Pringle stared at him. 'It was lost.'

'I know. That's the point. If it could be found I believe we might have the answer to the whole miserable business. Do you know the story of that ring? Where it came from, what its value was? Or anything which might point to where it is?'

For a moment he feared that he had been too headlong. But surprise gave place to resolution on Miss Pringle's face. The fact was, she was glad to have a chance to talk about Alan Bastable.

For a moment she twiddled a bit of cress between two fingers. She put it down and patted her hands with a paper table-napkin. Then she turned to Davie and said, 'Yes, I can tell you the story of the ring, Dr Davie. I've never told anyone else because it was a secret, but now that Florence and Alan are both gone, I don't suppose it matters. It hadn't struck me till now that it might be important.'

'I'm sure it is,' said Davie.

'You see,' began Miss Pringle, choosing her words slowly 'to begin with, you see, I had known Florence Bastable for years, and it was because Alan had known me since he was a boy that he came here as a student. He'd always wanted to be an actor, though he did try being a businessman first, and made a mess of it. That was why he was a bit older than some of them.'

'But the ring,' said Davie. 'Why was Miss Bastable so keen that he should have his father's ring?'

Miss Pringle looked at him in amazement. 'You know something about this already?'

'No. I've read the will, that's all. "The ring that his father gave me." Do you know why, or when, or where?'

XVI

'Are you sure you ought to do this, Alan?' said Mr Bullen. They were sitting in the manager's office in a doll's house of a bank in the High Street of Purton. Purton was just big enough to have a bank, and the bank was just small enough to look right in Purton.

'They're no heirlooms,' said Alan Merton.

'No, they're not. They're yours. I know that. But will your mother be happy about your taking the ring?'

'No, certainly she won't be. Up to last summer everything was hers to command. And she can't accommodate herself to the idea that things have changed. And of course she won't entertain for a moment the possibility of my getting married. I don't want to upset her, but I am not going to be dictated to by the family. So, please, I want to see the jewellery, Mr Bullen. And I'm going to choose a ring.'

'I suppose it's for—'

'Yes, it is.'

'You are on your rights, Alan. I wouldn't have said a word if I hadn't known you so many years.'

'Thank you, Mr Bullen. You've always been kind to me. I am grateful.'

And so presently Alan Merton reviewed the Merton Jewels, and chose the ring that he thought would look best on Florence's finger. It had a deep red stone and he thought it would look beautiful against her dark hair. If it would keep her sweet, his mother could have all those awful diamonds. He only wanted the ring with the red stone.

'You must sign for it, Alan,' said Mr Bullen. 'And for God's sake be careful of it. There's nothing so easily lost as a ring. People take them off to wash their hands and leave them all over the place. And in winter fingers shrink and rings slip off. And women pull them off inside their gloves in a most remarkable manner. They're better in banks. Better still in shops. And, by the way, you'll have to get it re-insured if you're taking it away. That is, if you're giving it away,' he added, with a sigh of responsibility.

'I'll take care. Thank you for your advice and help.'

And then the youthful 2nd Lieutenant Alan Merton shook hands with Mr Bullen, and presently departed up the High Street towards the railway station, which today is a silent ruin, but in 1944 was a stopping place twice a day for the slow train to London.

It was May, the gardens behind the station were bright with

lilac, and Alan Merton was feeling like a basket of flowers as he boarded the train.

Arrived in London, he went straight to a reputable jeweller and engaged him to cut a brief inscription on the inside of the ring. Then he went home and told his mother what he had done.

Lady Merton was aghast. 'You can't have taken that ring, Alan! You couldn't be such a fool!'

'I can and I have and I am,' said Alan.

'Don't agitate yourself, Frances,' said Aunt Hetty when she heard about it later. 'If he marries the gal the ring will stay in the family.'

'*If* he marries the girl!' cried Lady Merton. 'I pray to God he doesn't. Why, she's nothing but—'

That was the night that Alan slipped away to London to say goodbye. In his pocket he carried a jeweller's miniature box.

It was difficult to know how best to spend the evening. So much to say, so little time to say it in. They went to a restaurant in Soho which was able to produce something approximating to dinner. Then they walked home in the gathering darkness. Back at the flat, they did not draw the black-out curtains, or light the lamp. As they sat together in the window, Alan took the little box from his pocket, opened it with innocent pride, and placed the ring on her finger.

Caught by the moon the red stone glowed in the darkness.

'Oh, it's lovely!' said Florence. 'It's a garnet, isn't it?'

'There are words inside the ring,' said Alan in a whisper. 'You are not to read them till tomorrow—after I've gone.'

Till tomorrow—after I've gone.

That was the true story of Alan Bastable's ring. Of course, Miss Pringle did not know it in that form, but only as a collection of memories which Florence Bastable had confided to her.

'That was the end of his leave,' said Miss Pringle. 'He went to France on June 6th. Two days later he was killed. All Florence had of Alan's was the ring. I believe the family made some effort to get it back, but Florence would never give it up. She used to wear it on a chain round her neck, inside her dress. Nobody knew she had it—except one or two. I knew,' said Miss Pringle.

'And Alan?' asked Davie after a pause. 'Alan Bastable?'

'Alan was born the following January,' said Miss Pringle. 'I remember it as though it were yesterday.'

XVII

On Thursday at half past eleven Davie set off for Somerset House. This time he took a No. 9 bus from Piccadilly. He thought the pavements would be too crowded for long walking.

One in the left hand room, one in the right, his certificates were waiting for him. He sat down in the lobby of the Marriage room to examine them.

These things are admirably plain. The Marriage certificate consists in two lines of facts, one for the man, one for the woman. Harriet was registered as Harriet Orton, spinster, student, daughter of Joseph Orton, jeweller. Alan Bastable was registered as bachelor, student, son of Alan Merton, Army officer. Davie turned to the Birth certificate. There Alan had been registered only as the son of Florence Bastable. No father was recorded. Alan had taken advantage of the modern custom in the marriage certificate. You can put the father's name down if you know it. But Alan had stuck to Bastable for himself. That was sense. That was the name by which he was known—and it was a better name for the stage, so Davie thought.

Davie got up, stuffed the certificate in his pocket, and stepped into the Strand. Presently he boarded a No. 15 bus, intending to enjoy the London scene. But his mind was not with it.

He was more than ever interested in the ring. After hearing Miss Pringle's story he could not doubt that the Merton ring was valuable, that it was no garnet. What was not obvious was who would necessarily have known this.

Maybe the murderer had got loaded with the ring simply because he dare not throw it away—in which case he would have thrown it away somewhere else later on.

Maybe the murderer had not thrown it away, but still had no notion of its value. For half a minute he recalled the sight of Ian Rammage, seen in the looking-glass beside his ring in the crowded dressing-room at Renton's. Surely he couldn't be such a fool. But Alan Bastable's ring had looked fairly theatrical when he had seen it during the show at Winston Manor. It was that kind of ring, certainly.

Or maybe the murderer did know the value of the stone—in which case, whom could that involve? The Merton family? After all these years? Florence Bastable had concealed her ring: but other people besides Davie might have consulted her will. The ring had recently become "available", as it were.

Which of those possibilities fitted best with the theory he had formed in his heart?

The bus just then describing a powerful turn to the left, Davie looked down from his seat on the top deck, and perceived that they were already turning out of Piccadilly Circus into Regent Street. That was all right with him. He was prepared to go nearly as far as Oxford Circus.

The fact was that he had resolved upon a visit to Carnaby Street. He wanted to investigate those trousers.

XVIII

At three o'clock the following afternoon Edward Pomeroy poked his head round the office door and appealed to Miss Pringle's efficiency. 'Priscilla, I want to get on to Tito. I've dialled three times and nothing happens. Can you find out why?'

'I can ask the exchange,' said Miss Pringle, privately thinking that Edward could equally well have done that himself.

155

'Do,' said Mr Pomeroy.

'The answer,' said Miss Pringle three minutes later, 'is what you might expect. The line is out of order.'

'Oh, blow that!' said Pomeroy. 'I want to get Tito back. I can understand his not having wanted to work here this term, but surely he'll come back now. I can't go round to see him: I've got to meet that awful students' union in about a quarter of an hour.'

'And,' said Miss Pringle, quizzing her large desk engagement book, 'you've got the man from the Council at four.'

'Yes,' said Pomeroy, drumming on his hand with the end of a biro. 'I don't want to lose Tito. Could you spare the time to go round, Priscilla?'

'Now?'

'Yes.'

It was the last thing Miss Pringle wanted to do. But her reputation for total reliability was dear to her. She said she would go.

'I only want you to tell him that I wish he'd come back for the summer term. He *must* come back in September. But I'd like him here in May. There's nothing to discuss. If he comes he just does his stuff as usual—in the way he likes to do it.'

'Very well,' said Miss Pringle. 'I'll go right away. But I don't believe he'll do it.'

'Why not?'

'He was pretty shaken by the affair in November.'

'We all were.'

'And now Harriet's living with him.'

'I didn't know that.'

'I didn't either, till a few days ago. Apparently she's been there about two months.'

'I don't really see why that should influence him.'

'I'll see what he has to say,' said Miss Pringle. 'I expect he'll be in. Renton's is closed on Saturday.'

So Miss Pringle set off down the drive and walked thoughtfully along Merton Road. All the morning she had been thinking of Dr

Davie's telephone call. She had been gratified at the time, pleased to be consulted in so grave a matter. But she had soon realised that she had nothing to contribute, which had been rather deflating. And that naturally had stimulated dangerous speculations. She felt she *ought* to think of something: and that was how Miss Pringle began suspecting everyone. She had been thinking about it all the morning. She knew she was being scandalously unjust but she could not help herself. Peter Niccolini, Edward Pomeroy himself, Derek Wynter, Mrs Goode—none of them had escaped Miss Pringle's scrutiny. And now, here she was going to call on Harriet and Tito. She could not evade this mystery. Except for a moment at the theatre on Monday night, she had not seen either of them since November. It was, it would be, embarrassing.

Miss Pringle turned left. There still were gardens in Howarth Gardens. For some reason or other the railings had not been collected during the early nineteen forties to be turned into munitions, thus preserving for posterity a mass of gloomy evergreens, which had perhaps been planted in about 1910.

Time was when Edwardian tenants had taken an interest in their private pleasance. There had been gardeners. The lawn had been trimly kept. Now the garden was indifferently tended, and was visited in the day-time only by women with prams. Sometimes on warm summer nights, there were other visitors, for there was a way in through a broken railing, and the garden was a famous place of resort for the amorous young. But naturally Miss Pringle knew nothing of that. For her the garden looked sad. In the centre, beyond the shrubs, there were some fine trees, chestnuts, pink and white, and one noble tree whose branches swept the ground like a vast crinoline. That, thought Miss Pringle, must have been planted at least two hundred years ago, must have been there when Sir William Button lived at Winston Manor, and someone else, perhaps, had lived in another great house near by.

Instantly Miss Pringle was transported in the spirit. Trit-trot, down a long leafy lane, she saw Sir William on a sleek chestnut mare, dressed in his best, for he was to call at The Hall to ask if he might pay his addresses to Lavinia, only daughter of Sir George and Lady Howarth. (Surely that was the name.) Or better, thought Miss Pringle, improving on her theme, Sir William was probably not Sir William then. It was young Ensign William Button, *having been refused permission* (that was it) to pay his addresses to Lavinia, who was on his way down the leafy lane for a private assignation with the lady of his hopes, beside this lovely weeping tree in a secret corner of the park.

Where romance was concerned Miss Pringle's invention knew no limits, excepting those of actual time and place, which now informed her that she had walked past No. 17 Amelia Gardens. Perhaps it had been a definite subconscious attempt to evade an unwelcome mission. Plainly it could not succeed. 'Oh goodness!' said Miss Pringle, retracing her footsteps, while all her misgivings welled up again in her heart. She did hope Harriet would not say anything embarrassing.

And then she was standing on the step of No. 17, surveying a panel of bells to the right of the doorway. The top one (which was Swine and Minx's) bore no name. Next came Spinage Prendergast. Then (that was the first floor) came Adriano. The bottom bell was Madrigal. Miss Pringle rang Adriano, and as the front door was not shut, she entered the hall, walked up the stairs, and arrived outside Tito's door just as he opened it. He was wearing an overall and was carrying a paint brush in his hand.

'Hullo, Priscilla! How nice to see you. Come in.'

'What are you up to? Decorating?'

'Not exactly—with this sort of brush. I'm painting a picture of Harriet.'

'Then I'm interrupting—'

'Not a bit. I've been at it since lunch.'

'Is it permitted to see?'

'Oh yes.'

Harriet was seated on a throne on one side of the wide window. Tito's easel was on the other side. The room was no studio, but the window did face the right way for the light.

Harriet was wearing a black lace dress, a high comb in her black hair, a black mantilla. And in this darkness burned the garnets that she loved—at her ears two fiery drops, around her neck a double row of glowing red, and on the fingers of her right hand three more points of light.

'Don't move an inch, Harriet,' said Miss Pringle. 'You look lovely.'

'If only we could behave in a seventeenth century manner,' said Tito, 'and just walk around looking lovely, how elevating that would be.'

'But we can't,' said Miss Pringle. 'We have to go shopping, and make beds and put out the rubbish.'

Harriet said nothing. She seemed concerned to maintain her pose, one hand outstretched across her breast, the other hand palm upwards in her lap.

Miss Pringle turned to look at the canvas. It was a study in black, illuminated by Harriet's pale face and all those glowing stones. She had often seen scenery designed by Tito, but she had never seen a picture of his. It was a revelation. A revelation of Tito's ability, and, thought Miss Pringle, a revelation of Harriet. Beautiful certainly, but cold and proud and ruthless. She was, she suddenly thought, exactly like Vittoria, Vittoria in the play, the White Devil herself. Harriet would have looked the part much better than either Jane or Clarissa, who were simple little things from the North Country who would not willingly have said boo to a goose. 'It really is lovely,' said Miss Pringle. Too many rings looked vulgar on most people, but there on the canvas was Harriet with five points of fire on her fingers (for in the picture her other hand was turned the other way). She looked like a duchess, or perhaps (Miss Pringle mended her comparison) perhaps like the mistress of a duke. Miss Pringle could not take her eyes away.

'Well?' said Harriet. 'What are you staring at?'

'Just you.'

'Tito's idea of me,' said Harriet, breaking her pose. 'Tito, can I have a rest while you talk to Priscilla?'

'All right. You might make us some tea.'

'Not for me,' said Miss Pringle. 'I've only got two words to say, and then I must get back.'

'For us then,' Tito called after Harriet. 'Now, Priscilla.'

'Edward wants you to come back. He thinks your *commedia* work is essential. He understands why you wanted to get away, but he hopes you'll come back next term. He'd have said all this himself only your telephone's out of order—did you know?'

'No, I didn't. I hadn't meant to come back, Priscilla, but it's nice to know one's wanted.'

'You are, Tito. I promise you that.'

'Half a minute while I look at my little book,' said Tito, disappearing into the hall.

Miss Pringle returned to the portrait. Certainly, as a likeness, and in detail, it was remarkable—Vittoria Accoramboni to her fingertips. She stood there gazing at the picture, quite fascinated by it.

Presently, when she turned away, it was disconcerting to find that Harriet had been watching her from the bedroom door. She had taken off her dramatic dress, and all the jewellery except her earrings.

'Oh!' said Miss Pringle. 'I didn't realize you were there.'

'What are you so interested in?' asked Harriet.

Actually Miss Pringle had been studying Harriet's hands, but now she felt she had been complimentary enough. Harriet was sufficiently conceited already. She said, 'I'd no idea Tito was such a fine artist.'

'Nonsense,' said Tito, returning to the room. 'Tell Edward I'll do it—provided it's the same hours.'

'You shall have it exactly as you want,' said Miss Pringle. 'Edward will be delighted.'

'Bother you, Harriet,' said Tito. 'What have you undressed for?'

'I'm finished, Tito,' replied Harriet. 'Two hours at a go is enough. And I've just remembered I ought to go up to the school to see Derek Wynter about those fees. Now I've been to the place once I can go again. I shall walk back with Priscilla.'

'And what about my tea?'

'*You* can make that,' said Harriet.

Tito opened the door for them. As they walked down the stairs and past the ground floor flat they could hear Miss Madrigal singing 'Less than the dust beneath thy chariot wheels'. In an ecstasy of abasement her voice pursued them to the door. 'Even less am I, even less am I.'

The two women turned down Howarth Gardens and the singing faded on the air, leaving a silence that Miss Pringle did not welcome. She had never had much to say to Harriet. She had nothing at all to say to her now. Nor had Harriet anything much to say to her, though once or twice she had looked at Priscilla rather hard, as though she would have liked to ask her some question.

'Are you going to the office?' asked Harriet when they reached the drive.

'In a minute,' said Miss Pringle, 'but first of all I'm going to have that cup of tea I didn't have with you.'

'See you some time,' said Harriet.

Miss Pringle turned down the path to the theatre. The garden was very quiet. A few students were sitting on the grass. Others might be attending classes in the studio. But it was the last week of term. There was nothing doing.

The canteen was empty but for the attendant, Maureen. So Miss Pringle sat down alone and was glad to do that, because she had strange thoughts in her head, and had had ever since Dr Davie had claimed her confidence. In her experience a cup of tea was the finest clearer of the head, the best steadier of the nerves, and prime comforter in all emergencies. And so she sat there, lost in thought, gazing into her tea-cup. Dr Davie's ideas had been so neatly presented, so logically argued. She ought to be able to do the same: but her thoughts were so peculiar and there was no one to discuss them with. It was frustrating.

Presently she got up and walked down the corridor towards the wardrobe. On the way back to the office she thought she would look in and ask Mrs Goode if she lacked anything before the holidays began.

As she approached she noticed that the wardrobe door was ajar, which was not usual. It was the accepted ritual to knock on the door, but, the door being open, Miss Pringle peeped inside, and was surprised to see nobody there. And then she was surprised by something else. All the light in the room seemed to be concentrated on Mrs Goode's table in the window, which sparkled in the sunshine, silver and gold, ruby, emerald, sapphire, and diamante. Mrs Goode had been sorting out her collection of theatrical jewellery. Even in daylight, even close to, it looked as though she were possessed of half the treasures of Baghdad.

Impelled by she knew not what, Miss Pringle stepped softly into the room and advanced towards the table. And 'Hi!' said a voice, 'I didn't hear you come in.'

It was a kind of rebuke.

Miss Pringle turned quickly towards the right and found herself regarding Mrs Goode's head and shoulders above a closely packed rack of clothes.

'The door wasn't shut,' explained Miss Pringle.

Mrs Goode, holding a ribbon of the Order of the Garter, stepped round the end of the rack and returned to her table. Placing the ribbon on the side of the table, she swept up some rings and put them in a box.

'I was just going over the jewellery,' she said. 'They like to hang on to it if they can. That's why I keep a list. They ought really to provide their own, but they know I've got some effective pieces and they ask for them. And I can't say no.'

'Yes,' said Miss Pringle. 'You've got to be careful.'

'Anything I've not got tonight I won't get at all.'

'No,' said Miss Pringle, 'I don't suppose you will.'

She was feeling stupid. She had only meant to say hullo, but she had looked as though she were snooping, and she thought Mrs Goode had not liked it. 'I just looked in to see if you were all right,' she said. 'If you're wanting to make any claims, or anything, I'll be glad to know.'

'I've no claims,' said Mrs Goode.

'O.K. Then I must be getting on,' said Miss Pringle.

She was glad to get out. Mrs Goode had not been at all in her usual humour: more like a miser counting his treasures than the genial Mrs G. It had been a strange encounter.

Miss Pringle hastened back to the house. At the top of the stairs she paused and looked about her. Edward Pomeroy's door was shut. So was Derek Wynter's. Miss Pringle stepped softly to the bursary door and listened. She could hear nothing. Then she crossed to Mr Pomeroy's door and listened. He was talking to somebody. It was probably the man from the Council.

Miss Pringle slipped into her office and closed the door quietly. She was feeling unpleasantly agitated. The whole afternoon had been extremely uncomfortable. And especially disquieting had been an information which had accidentally revealed itself to Miss Pringle without a word spoken. Dr Davie had asked her to let him know at once if she had anything to report. And surely she had. But ought she to do it? Could she be mistaken? Was it disloyal? The temporising questions raced through her mind. And should she write or telephone? Miss Pringle, a nervous finger at her lips, could not decide. The telephone would be quicker, and speed was important: at least, she supposed it was.

It was several minutes before she could make up her mind, but at last she put out her hand to the telephone, and rather gingerly put her finger on the dial. Even then it would have been a relief if the number had been engaged. But it was not.

'The Chesterfield Club.'

'Is Dr Davie in, please?'

'No, madam, he isn't. He went out just now. He said he wouldn't be in till after six.'

There was the anti-climax.

'Oh . . . Could I leave a message?'

'Certainly, madam.'

'Then will you please tell Dr Davie that Miss Pringle rang up and that it's important. I am going back to my flat now. I will ring up at six, or perhaps, if he comes in earlier, he would ring me. Yes, he does know my number. Please say it's important.'

As she cradled the telephone the room seemed suddenly quiet. Had she been talking very loudly? She opened her door, and listened: and thought she heard a distant creak on the stair. She crossed the landing and peered over the banister. She could see no one. Returning to the office she looked out of the window. Mrs Goode was walking down the drive. A number of students, Harriet among them, were standing round the main entrance, talking. And then Derek Wynter came out of the front door and joined them. It might have been any of them. Oh Lord, thought Miss Pringle, it might have been no one. I'm nervous.

Presently she went to Mr Pomeroy's door. There was no one talking now. What a fool I am, she thought: it was probably the Councillor going down stairs. She gave a little knock on the door and opened it without waiting for an answer.

Edward Pomeroy was standing by the window, his face towards her. He looked tired and worried, even cross. Evidently, thought Miss Pringle, the interview with the Councillor had been unfruitful.

'I've been to Tito,' she began.

'And?'

'And he'll do it.'

'Good.'

'If there's nothing else, Edward, I'll be going now. I've got a date tonight,' said Miss Pringle with slight exaggeration.

'Lucky you,' said Edward Pomeroy. He made no effort to detain her.

It was past five o'clock. She collected her bag, walked down stairs, submitted herself to the amiable badinage of the young, and then walked down the drive and Merton Road and stationed herself at the bus stop by the Green Dragon.

It was only a short drive to Crofton Mansions. She would have to wait at home for perhaps half an hour before she could call Dr Davie. But she must be there because of course he might come in earlier. *He* might ring *her*.

When the bus drew up it was rather full. It always was full at that time of day. But Miss Pringle managed to get a seat on top. For a few seconds she was concerned with the business of sitting down. Then she was back with her problem.

Oh God, said Miss Pringle to her heart, I can't be wrong. I'd know that ring anywhere.

.

PART FOUR

THE MASK

I

I T W A S F I V E - T H I R T Y when Miss Pringle reached Crofton
Mansions. It was an old block of flats, and there was no lift.
Miss Pringle's flat was on the third floor, and three flights of
stairs is a long way up.

Always, as she mounted, Miss Pringle noticed the same things.
First, the green dado, which she disliked. Then, the staircase
window with its outlook on to a court like a well, paved, dark, a
lonely sycamore in the centre. She disliked that too. Then the
names: Pill and Wyznerz on the first floor: Fountain and Cold
on the second. She knew Miss Fountain, but the others she did
not know even by sight. In London it takes years to recognize a
neighbour.

Miss Pringle had got to know Miss Fountain over a matter of
window-boxes. One evening, two years before, when Miss
Pringle was bending over her box of fuchsias, petunias, and
tumbling lobelias, Miss Fountain had chanced to put her head
out of her window to investigate her culinary herbs. She had
collected a surprising number of the smaller fragrances, and took
great pleasure in their encouragement.

It was at this moment when Miss Fountain was bending over
her aerial garden that Miss Pringle had gaily drained a jug of
water over her flowers, and had heard with dismay a sudden
affronted cry from the window below. She had felt so guilty that
she had run downstairs and tapped on Miss Fountain's door,
partly, perhaps, to forestall any retaliatory action which Miss
Fountain might be contemplating, but partly from genuine con-
cern. And from that hour Miss Fountain and Miss Pringle had
been sworn sisters, the trusted guardians of each other's latch

keys, the friendly dispensers of minor groceries in times of improvidence.

The flight to the third floor seemed always longer and steeper than the others, but there at last she was. Pringle, the door on the left. That on the right concealed Miss Binge. Concealed was the word, for propinquity had not ripened into acquaintance with Miss Binge. Miss Binge was a mystery character. In many ways it was good to live next door to a silent and invisible neighbour. But it was rather like living next door to a ghost. Sometimes Miss Pringle wished that Miss Binge would throw a party, do something to deserve her name.

Miss Pringle let herself in. The letter-boxes were downstairs so there was never the interest of finding an envelope on the mat. Or even a coupon allowing two pence off something or other which she had no intention of buying: coupon-pushers could not be bothered to climb three flights of stairs. Wherein they were wise: they would not have hooked Miss Pringle, who was constitutionally incapable of entering a shop and demanding something at a reduced price, coupon or not.

Miss Pringle put down her bag and went into the bathroom to wash her hands and pat her hair into shape. Then she entered the sitting-room, opened a small cupboard in a remarkably small sideboard, and poured herself out a fiery glass of South African sherry. She did not really like sherry very much, or not this sherry, but she liked a little something, and gin was so expensive. Whisky she had not seriously considered. Solitary whisky drinking would not have been at all in Miss Pringle's character.

She sat down in the armchair and was reminded, as always, that it was too small. The edge caught you half way along the thigh. In Miss Pringle's judgement a proper armchair ought to be three feet long in the seat: but that was something you never saw in the kind of furniture shop that suited her income.

She took a sip of sherry, and returned to her anxiety. She wished Dr Davie would ring *her*, and sooner than six. She wanted to get rid of her information, get rid of it before it hurt her. Already she could see complications. Already she was half-regretting she had rung him up. She did not want to make trouble, but surely trouble was exactly what might follow.

She put down her glass, got up, and crossed to the window. There was nothing to please there. Her box was not yet arrayed for summer. She turned back to the room, considered a moment, and then went into the kitchen. The necessary thing was to *do* something. It was no good making *Quiche Lorraine*, as she had originally intended, or even a macaroni cheese, because if the telephone rang in the middle something appalling would happen. She made a custard pudding, and put it in a *bain marie*, and set the regulator at No. 1. No harm could come of that. Then she went back to the sitting-room. The clock on the mantel-shelf was pointing to ten minutes to six. Miss Pringle walked over to the window and inspected the window-box again. It had not altered.

Then she sat down at her bureau. This again was too small. In the good days of furniture-making an open bureau had presented a surface like a small table—something to put your elbows on: but these little lady-like things were absurd—like something exquisitely useless at Versailles, but not of that quality. It was all right to keep things in, but no one could comfortably write anything longer than a signature at it. She hunched herself over the open flap and took a writing-pad out of a pigeon-hole. She wanted to make a few notes. When Dr Davie rang she wanted to say what she had to say without fumbling for words.

She started to write, and twenty seconds later the door bell rang.

'Oh, drat it!' said Miss Pringle under her breath. It was five minutes to six. Dr Davie might ring at any time. It would be awkward if anyone else were in the flat. She wished she had one of those peep-holes in her door. Of course, if it were Jill Fountain—but Jill usually gave two rings close together.

The bell rang again. Miss Pringle got up, and walked slowly to the hall. It was not in her nature to refuse to answer a bell.

She opened the door.

And 'Hullo!' said Miss Pringle, greatly surprised. 'I couldn't think who it could be—'

And then the telephone began to ring. Everything was happening at once.

'Sorry,' said Miss Pringle. 'I must answer that awful thing. Come on into the sitting-room. I won't keep you waiting long.'

But as it turned out, Miss Pringle was detained much longer than she expected. Her visitor decided not to wait. And although Dr Davie rang her up at a quarter past six, half past six and twenty to seven, he still could get no answer.

11

George Canteloupe smiled his amusement from his seat in the bar as Davie rejoined him for the third time in the space of twenty-five minutes.

'I hope you realize R.V. that this display of tireless activity can gain no possible applause.'

Davie slumped into his chair and found refuge by peering deeply into the contents of his wallet. 'And surely,' continued Canteloupe, 'a little more consideration is owed to the flagging constitution.'

'Flagging, George?' Davie felt a momentary hurt, but this was because he had been taken off guard. His mind had been preoccupied with speculation as to the reasons for Miss Pringle's message. And, in reparation of his apparent lapse in good humour, Davie broached a smile.

'I see. Compassion for my great antiquity.' Davie laughed outright. He then withdrew from his wallet a ticket for that evening's performance at the Coliseum and placed it purposefully on the table beside him.

'It's probably too late to be of the slightest use to anyone, but it seems I am unable to go myself. If it would not be too great an imposition, would you try to pass it on? It's *Carmen*.'

'All right, I'll do my best. But that means you're off again.'

'Forgive me, George. The truth is, I'm concerned for someone who may need my help and unless I am mistaken, the safari should leave at once.'

'My dear fellow, of course.'

Davie swallowed the last of his whisky, waved a farewell and made for the door.

Canteloupe picked up the opera ticket, glanced at it wistfully for a moment, then waved it spiritedly in the air. 'Hang it, I'll go myself,' he called resolutely to Davie's retreating figure. 'And good hunting.'

Davie had already found Miss Pringle's address from the telephone directory and now wasted no time in getting a taxi to take him there.

III

Oblivious of the passing scene, he was swept northward across Oxford Street in the direction of St. Marylebone, whilst his thoughts were concentrated on the elusiveness of Miss Pringle.

There was no very satisfactory explanation for her failure to answer the telephone on all *three* occasions, he told himself. If she had been unable to wait, why had she not rung again before six? After all, she was a meticulous, trustworthy and eminently reliable sort of person. A person for whose help he was already much indebted. The message had been that she was on her way home with the intention of ringing him again at six. The message had also been for him to ring her if he returned earlier. And, although she had repeated with emphasis that the matter was important, it now appeared that something of even greater urgency had detained her. Could it be . . . ?

Anxiety mounted within him. And, just as his heartbeat began to quicken, the wheels of the taxi were squeezed to a halt outside Crofton Mansions.

He climbed the steps and hurried into the hallway. No key of names was in evidence. Foolishly he had neglected to take careful note of Miss Pringle's flat number, so he would have to check the flats individually. On the ground floor were "Rotter" and "Osobase". On the first "Wyznerz" and "Pill". He swallowed heavily as he began his next ascent. After a pause for breath on the second floor, he made obeisance to the door marked "Fountain" at which moment a female vóice called out a challenge from behind him. 'Are you looking for someone?'

'Ah! Yes I am. Do you happen to know of a Miss Pringle?'

'Certainly I do,' came the cheerful reply. 'It's not much further. Number Seven, immediately above me. I live here.' said the claimant to Number Five, eyeing him as she attempted to fit the key into the door with indifferent success. 'I think you should find her in at this time,' she smiled coyly. 'But, of course, you will be expected.' She blinked.

'No. Not exactly. At least, she was expecting me to be in touch, but I've had the greatest difficulty in my attempts to get her on the telephone.'

'Oh! Well, I expect she will be home now. But if not, and you would like to leave a message or anything, just give me a buzz here. Fountain is the name.'

'How kind. Thank you.'

Four minutes later, Davie had returned to Miss Fountain's door and given the necessary buzz. The response was unexpectedly immediate.

'Oh dear! No luck?' she enquired.

'I'm afraid not.'

Miss Fountain bowed and inclined her head in sympathy.

'Perhaps she is calling on someone else in the block. Has she a particular friend, do you know?'

'Not to my knowledge. That is, apart from me.' And she searched his face for any flicker of approval.

'In that case,' said Davie, 'I had better explain. Miss Pringle left me a message to expect a telephone call from her at six o'clock this evening on a matter of grave importance. But I heard nothing more. I tried to ring back, of course, but without success.'

'Oh, what a shame. I'm so sorry.' But then Miss Fountain grasped the further implication of Davie's explanation.

'Wait!' she said. 'I know just what to do. I keep a duplicate key to her front door. We had better look, in case she has been taken ill or something dreadful. I won't be a minute.'

Miss Fountain re-emerged and took five or six frisky skips to the top of the stairs and unlocked the door of Miss Pringle's flat.

'I say,' she called, 'that's very odd. She has left something on.'

A few moments later, Davie reached the half open door of Number Seven. He noticed the smell of cooking. He saw Miss Fountain leave the kitchen and move across the passage.

'I'll just take a peep in the sitting-room.' She knocked and called out, 'Priscilla . . . Pris-cil-la!' There was utter silence. She opened the door and went in. Davie heard her cry out, 'Oh quick, come quickly.'

IV

Davie found Miss Pringle lying face downwards on the far side of the room. There was a wound in her back, just below the left shoulder blade, from which blood was still seeping. He took her pulse; there was no movement. He asked Miss Fountain, partly for her own sake, to go downstairs and telephone the police, whilst he remained to make sure nothing was touched.

Poor, poor Miss Pringle. For once in his life, Davie felt intense anger. Why, *why* should anyone kill this gentle inoffensive creature; this conscientious, kindly soul? But he already knew the answer: he recalled the voice of George Canteloupe at the Club, 'The preventive murderer. The chap who murders the man with the evidence.' Now he knew that this must be so and a sense of guilt bore down upon him. It was through his actions that an innocent person had become thus involved. But he would not allow this emotion to cloud his judgement. He had told himself many times before that the citizen owed a responsibility to his fellows and this condition must, of necessity, include some dangers. He would not blame himself too much.

Davie turned over in his mind the succession of events which had led him to his conclusions. He had approached Miss Pringle for possible evidence, but at the time she had been unable to provide any details to further his investigation. It seemed to him now that she must have subsequently stumbled upon some new fact connected with the Alan Bastable affair and that somehow her murderer had known of her discovery. It also seemed to him that the purpose of Miss Pringle's telephone call to the Chesterfield had been to get rid of her information but that her attempt had been narrowly thwarted.

While he thought this out, Davie was beginning to take in the details of the flat. Miss Pringle lay between the back of the Chelsea sofa and the telephone table, which was in the far corner. By the window at the opposite end of the room stood a small bureau with an open flap supporting writing materials. The distance between the upright chair and the bureau suggested that Miss Pringle had been interrupted—possibly by a telephone call—conceivably by his own. He noticed also the solitary, unfinished drink—her visitor had been unexpected, then.

Davie went across to the small bureau and saw the open note-pad. Miss Pringle was indeed efficient. Here was evidence— the evidence so long denied him. How bitterly ironical; Miss Pringle had already noted down what she intended to tell him, and the murderer had killed in vain.

When the police arrived, Davie was standing at the window, deep in thought. He knew now what he must do. 'If you are shortly returning to the station, he said, I will accompany you. I am anxious to make a statement.'

V

Tito put a final brush stroke to his canvas. 'There,' he called with justifiable satisfaction, 'it's finished.'

'Oh, do let me see.' Harriet ran to his side and stood in admiration of the face gazing back at her. 'Oh, Tito, it's magnificent.'

'Well, I would say—a true likeness.' She was not conscious of any irony. He gathered his brushes and attempted to clean the paint stains from his hands. 'It will hang in my Autumn exhibition for all to admire. You'd like that.'

'Oh yes, I'd adore it, Tito.'

Tito stretched himself and yawned. 'I'm far too exhausted to cook now. Look, it's already eight o'clock. We'll go out for a meal. I feel like celebrating.'

Harriet hugged him passionately. 'Lovely! But give me time to get ready.'

Exotic odours wafted from the bathroom. Harriet was now enjoying release from anxiety as she lay in the foam and began to reflect upon her good fortune. Her life with Tito promised interest and gaiety. He was highly talented and had already achieved enviable success. He would take her far, of this she was quite certain. And then, who knows?

It was a pity about Priscilla. But it was her own fault, she should not have interfered. There was no doubt that when she came round that afternoon and scrutinized the portrait, she had recognized the ring—her beautiful ring. Harriet had been quite unable to resist wearing it when posing for her portrait. And Tito, with his total lack of interest in jewellery, would not know it from one of Mrs Goode's stage props. Anyway, he was hopelessly vague about some things. But Priscilla knew the ring, and she was no fool.

If only Priscilla could have been persuaded to hold her tongue. But no: as soon as they had arrived at Winston's together, she had left the theatre and slipped back into the office to telephone that old prodnose Davie. Fortunately, it had been possible to overhear her—and the gist of her message. It had been unexpectedly easy to follow her home and prevent her from answering the telephone.

Harriet congratulated herself. She knew she had been lucky. But then, she had also managed to keep her nerve. Yes, she had done well. And now, with Priscilla out of the way, no one else from Winston Manor would be allowed close enough to identify the ring as being the one Alan used to wear. Harriet would see to that. She had wanted that ring more than anything in the world, and it had been perfectly beastly of Alan not to give it to her or even to let her wear it sometimes. Worse, he had deceived her into expecting a comfortable inheritance, yet there had been nothing. But she did not care so much now about the money. She had the ring—the ring was hers at last. She had recognized its value from the very beginning. She had always been fascinated by jewellery and from her father she had learnt to distinguish between what was valuable and what was not. Alan's ruby was very valuable indeed, and in this, too, he had tried to deceive her. Added to that, he had soon made it plain that he found Harriet insufficient: he was a womanizer. Had he really supposed that she was prepared to play second fiddle? Even now she winced when she recalled her humiliation.

Of course, she had to get rid of him: equally of course she had to punish him.

The means to both ends had presented itself when she was turning over the contents of Priscilla's handbag in the office, and had seen the wardrobe key among the other clutter in the drawer of the desk. Priscilla would not notice the temporary absence of the key: she never had occasion to use it unless Mrs Goode was away.

The plan, conceived in a flash, had gone without a hitch.

Harriet had gone from the office into the garden and into the theatre by the side door. The show had begun and Mrs Goode was in the auditorium as usual. There was no one to see Harriet letting herself into wardrobe, conveniently opposite the O.P. door.

That Alan was playing Pantaloon was a gift: the duplicate costume enveloped her from neck to ankles, and the ridiculous sugar-loaf hat effectually concealed her hair. Harriet had surveyed herself with satisfaction in Mrs Goode's long looking glass: it was a perfect disguise, wanting only the mask to make it impenetrable.

She had watched so many rehearsals that she knew the business backwards and could have understudied any part at a moment's notice. Now the second act was under way, and everybody on the stage except Pantaloon. Alan would be waiting in the wings.

As she took the stiletto Harriet smiled. It was an heirloom from some Spanish ancestor, and when she had asked her father to give it to her he had laughed and said, 'Be careful, it's a lethal weapon.' That was why she had wanted it, and always carried it in her capacious handbag: the secret possession of it gave her an obscure satisfaction.

She had moved stealthily across the corridor and through the O.P. door. Alan stood with his back to her. As she raised her arm to strike, she had known a moment of regret: she wished he could have seen her, if only in that instant; revenge is sweeter if the victim recognizes the avenger.

He had given a little grunt as he fell, and she had snicked the ring from his finger and put it on her own almost before he crumpled to the floor. Then she had unfastened the mask and adjusted it over her face: it had been warm against her skin.

Lifting the body under the knees, she had humped it out of the way under a huddle of curtains behind the scenery. There had been a burst of laughter from the auditorium, and the Doctor's voice gave Harriet her cue.

Into the glow of the footlights stepped Pantaloon: there was more laughter. What a churlish unsociable old curmudgeon he was: he wouldn't even answer when spoken to, but sat hunched over his accounts, his gaudy ring flashing as he totted the columns of figures up and down, down and up. . . . Harriet had never given a better performance nor enjoyed one so much.

After her bath, Harriet felt much invigorated. Life had never seemed so good.

She was attending to her face when the front door bell rang. She heard Tito go into the hall, and the sound of male voices. Friends of his, she supposed. Damn! She hoped he would stop them from boring on and on: she was hungry.

She was applying lipstick when Tito put his head round the door.

'Two chaps asking to see you, Harriet. Police officers actually—they say there's been an accident—' He broke off in astonishment as she caught his wrist in a vice-like grip.

'You *bloody* fool!' she hissed. 'Why didn't you say I was out—?'

Tito was acquainted with the cat dormant in Harriet: he had not, till now, met the tigress. Her face was distorted with rage. Without relaxing her grip she hissed again, 'Keep them talking—do you understand?' Then, releasing him, she raised her voice so that it carried clearly and confidently. 'Right, Tito. I can't imagine what they want, but let me get some clothes on and I'll be with you in a trice.'

VI

With coat and handbag trailing behind her, Harriet was out of the back door and down the fire escape in seconds. She streaked across the garden, along the back alley and turned into the side road, where she paused for breath. No one was following, yet,

but she dared not stop for more than a moment. She braced
herself. The odds against her were mounting but she tossed back
her head defiantly. And on she raced along the pavement
until—there, across the road a car door was wide open. And
kneeling in the driver's seat a camping enthusiast was cramming
his paraphernalia into the back. Then, perhaps in need of more
supplies, he disappeared into the nearby block of flats. Harriet
seized her chance and darted for the open door. With the devil's
own luck, she found that the key had been left in the ignition.
She started the car and was off at speed into the main road. She
nosed her way ahead of the slow-moving traffic and then, in an
effort to beat the lights, she opened up full throttle. Tyres
screeched, horns blared as she weaved in and out—but she was
across. Swerving to miss an oncoming bus by inches, she raced
on. They weren't on her tail yet, but they would not be stalled
for long. Then with horror she remembered—*the ring*. God,
what a fool! Turn left here and—NO ENTRY. Hell! . . . supposing they searched? . . . Opposing vehicles bore down upon her
as they hooted in protest. There was no time to go back. The
moaning sound of an emergency horn could be heard behind her
in the distance. Somehow she must go on—she must. She
ploughed through the one-way street, mounting the curb and
grazing successive lamp posts, until at last she could turn off.
Left, then right and right again. She had lost all sense of
direction. All that mattered now was to keep going.

Harriet picked up speed again and took the next bend furi-
ously. As she did so, she noticed out of the corner of her eye the
flashing blue light of a police car in pursuit. GIVE WAY. She
braked violently, but too late. The car skidded into the major
road.

Above the fearful din of rending metal and splintering glass
came a single piercing shriek.

PART FIVE

CURTAIN

1

THAT AFTERNOON, DR DAVIE was to return to Cambridge. But he knew he must call on Edward Pomeroy and bid him farewell—this much he owed.

'I had to come—just to say "hello" and "goodbye" and how very sorry . . .'

'It's good of you to come Dr Davie and thank you. People have been most kind, really most kind. Won't you please sit down.'

Pomeroy perched himself on the edge of his chair and, with unseeing eyes, gazed across the desk at the floor beyond. As was to be expected, he appeared to be in a state of considerable shock and bewilderment.

'Of course, I'm not yet able to believe what has happened. It has been far too distressing for the mind to grasp all at once. Yet sooner or later one has to face the truth,' Pomeroy felt compelled to glance in the direction of Miss Pringle's door, 'and in spite of everything, life must somehow go on.' He fell silent. Davie became acutely aware of the empty office next door, and here, in his own bare room, Pomeroy seemed a lonely figure. 'I expect most of our students—the best ones at least—will find places in one of the other schools. But, as for me and my staff, I simply cannot imagine what will happen to us. As you know, the school has been my whole life.'

'One very good reason, perhaps, why it should continue to be. And another is your achievement. I have come to know some of your students quite well and I cannot believe they would desert you. On the other hand, to ask you to continue much as before, is to expect a great deal. But then, as you know, youth does expect a great deal. And, on the whole, I think you will not disappoint these young people. At their time of life, memories are short and soon clouded by the ever changing prospect of some new experience. Nowadays, they live almost entirely in the present and the immediate future, or so it seems to me.'

'You are probably quite right, Dr Davie, and I'm grateful to you for your encouragement. You sound as though you believe what we have been doing here has, after all, been worth-while. I may have allowed myself to become too despondent. Perhaps if we all have faith enough . . .'

'Ah! And there I must leave you. I return to Cambridge by an afternoon train and must first snatch a quick lunch.'

11

The hubbub of the Green Dragon was rather more than Davie cared for on this particular occasion and he had therefore found himself a secluded corner. A familiar voice called out cheerfully above the general commotion, 'Dr Davie. What a pleasant surprise.' Davie turned to see the smiling face of Martin Searle.

'Hello Martin, come and join me.'

'Thank you. You must wonder why I'm here after end of term. The truth is, I hoped there might be some chance of running into you.' Davie smiled. He was genuinely pleased to see this young man again.

'So it was Harriet.' Davie nodded his affirmation. 'May one know—do you mind my asking?—how did you discover the truth?'

'Of course you may ask. I am indebted to you for helping me to clarify my thoughts at a very difficult juncture.' Martin blushed with pleasure. 'But first we must order our lunch. I can recommend the cold beef, and the cheese and celery.'

III

'I followed the trails of too many red herrings,' said Davie, 'for which I reproach myself. I was not long deceived into thinking it was an outside job, but I was seriously misled by Mrs Goode's contention that the Doctor's costume had been moved, and the fact that a second Doctor had been seen off-stage that night.' Martin blushed again, and Davie added quickly, 'Your prank caused only a very temporary complication, though I admit at first that the probabilities pointed to a male member of the cast. No, Martin, you were never suspect. But Derek Wynter did come into my speculations.'

'Derek Wynter? The *Bursar*?' Martin was incredulous.

'The Bursar. I think he had a strong reason for wanting Alan Bastable out of the way. This, I must add, is speculation, not proven fact. I happened to see Bastable come out of the Bursar's office that evening when I was waiting on the landing for Edward Pomeroy. I also happened to see Derek Wynter's face when Alan had left him: it was the face of a man at the end of his tether.'

Martin looked even more incredulous. 'But what could Alan have said to upset Derek? Except for official matters they hardly knew each other.'

'Maybe. As I say, this is only conjecture. But I think Alan had a hold on Derek. Possibly Derek at some time borrowed privately from the school funds—and when I say borrowed, I don't put the word in inverted commas. I don't doubt Wynter's integrity. But in a difficult moment he may have helped himself temporarily, and Alan may have somehow discovered this and threatened to tell Pomeroy. So Derek was easy game and a source of income to Bastable.'

'You mean. . .' Martin laid down his knife and fork and stared at Davie, 'You mean Alan used *blackmail*?'

'Why not? Alan Bastable didn't have an over-sensitive conscience. Also, you must remember, he was hard-up—Harriet was an expensive luxury.

'But that is beside the point. It was when I realized that Mrs Goode might have been mistaken, and that it was Pantaloon's costume that had been borrowed, that I began to have an inkling. You see, if Alan had been killed at the end of the show, the disappearance of the ring, the fact that the mask was found beside the body, and the incontrovertible witness of the stop-watch just did not add up. It was barely conceivable that the murderer could have killed him in eighty seconds and made his get-away; it was *impossible* that he could have stayed to remove mask and ring in that space of time. And why should he remove the mask and ring? Was the object murder or robbery—or both? If both, who stood to gain? Who had a sufficiently strong motive for wanting simultaneously to get rid of Bastable and secure his ring? And why should the mask have been tampered with unless the murderer himself had used it?

'Once I had asked myself these questions, the answer was not far to seek. The ring in fact was not stolen. As you know, it was ultimately found in Mrs Bastable's jewel case. As Alan's lawful heir she had a right to it.'

'But it was Harriet who made such a noise about it being lost.'

'Yes. Clever, wasn't it. She was an actress, both on and off stage. The impersonation of Pantaloon presented no difficulties to her. She knew the business. All she had to do was to keep her nerve.

'I was puzzled by Peter Niccolini's statement that he had heard the O.P. door open during the last applause, but that when he looked out he had seen nobody in the corridor. But that too was later explained by the facts. Of course he saw no one: Harriet, having dropped the mask and retrieved the weapon, had only to sneak across into the wardrobe. It would have taken her next to no time at all.'

'But why did she go to these lengths? Surely, if she was sick of Alan, she would have had no scruples about divorce?'

'Certainly no scruples: but another sort of objection. She could only have got her divorce on the grounds of Alan's infidelity; and Harriet would have felt that to be a public humiliation. She was a jealous, revengeful, greedy woman. And on top of every reason for hatred, I think she saw the possibility of another woman winning that ring. The girl Laura had in fact worn it during rehearsal. I saw her put it on her finger. And so did Harriet Bastable. Harriet understood these things. She knew a genuine ruby when she saw one, and she did not intend to let it go.'

'I still don't quite see how you proved all this, Dr Davie.'

'I proved it by the ring. The chap who dressed with Bastable knew that ring, and knew that Bastable wore it that night. He was not wearing it when he was found. And my theory was ultimately confirmed by Miss Pringle. Poor Miss Pringle saw the ring: Harriet was wearing it when she posed for Tito, and Miss Pringle recognized it in the portrait. She left written evidence of this. She had asked me to telephone and she had made notes of what she intended to say. I found the paper on her bureau.'

'I'm afraid I'm being captious,' said Martin apologetically, 'but how were you so sure that it was the same ring? After all, Harriet had a lot of jewellery and always wore earrings and rings of sorts: there's a sameness about rings.'

'Not about this one,' and Davie told Martin the story of Alan's father and Florence Bastable. 'There was an engraving inside the ring, "To Florence with eternal love from Alan" and the date. It is nearly twenty-six years old. Only a few months older than young Alan Bastable.'

'I see—yes. And did the police find the weapon? It puzzled me at the time that it was never discovered.'

'Yes. The weapon in each case was a stiletto. It was found in Harriet's handbag near her body.'

Martin was silent, toying without appetite with his cheese and celery. Dr Davie went to the bar and returned with two brandies.

'The occasion, if not the lunch, warrants these,' he said.

'Thank you *Doctor*—the very finest restorative!' Martin sighed deeply. 'It has certainly been a harrowing affair and to have been part of it all, so to speak, gives one an extraordinary sense of what —inverted privilege?—which one can only contemplate with disbelief. Yet it is also something one can never quite forget. Never.'

Davie rolled his glass gently between his palms and peered deeply into it. 'No, we can never forget. But we must not brood. Now, no more of this. What you must turn to is the future, Martin. I believe you have a promising career ahead of you and I hope nothing will spoil it.'

'Well, I've been thinking that things might sort themselves out if I transferred to Renton's. But there is a difficulty because, over there, any originality or natural talent has to be sacrificed to the system. The emphasis is on conformity—every student inevitably becomes a near replica of the next.'

' "Vive la différence", n'est ce pas?'

Martin grinned appreciatively, 'I'm so glad you agree. At Winston Manor we indulge in experiment and we have the most magnificent disasters sometimes. And some of the staff . . .' He broke off. 'But I feel sorry for Edward. He has worked so hard to build the place up. Besides, he is a decent chap and I shouldn't like to let him down now. The truth is,' said Martin sheepishly, 'I've already decided. I shall stay with him.'

Davie was silent; but his smile was full of approval.

Davie collected his suitcase from the Chesterfield and was soon comfortably installed in a corner seat with his back to the engine on the three thirty-five from King's Cross. Normally, his interest would have been drawn towards the last-minute bustle of travellers—he was always susceptible to whatever little dramas might be enacted between carriage and platform. But now he felt unable to support the strain of emotional involvement and so withdrew behind his copy of the morning paper.

By the time the train had begun to draw away from the station, he had dispensed with the first two pages of news. Invariably he found the domestic front more engaging.

' "The Feetbeaters" return from their triumphal tour of the upper East Side of Manhattan.' All seats were sold for a special appearance in Brighton, prior to their departure for Australia next week. Good, no problem there. He would certainly *not* be among the swingers.

Oh! Calcutta! and *Hair* were still on. It seemed that the new vogue for abandonment was here to stay. But he considered it was high time *Pyjama Tops* came off—or, at least, that the bottoms be accounted for as soon as possible.

Aida Cowie tempted the gourmet from her cookery section with a majestic recipe for a *Pavlova*—a New Zealand speciality of choice fresh fruit and whipped cream wrapped in meringue-like base. Devastation upon the figure, one would think. Davie regretted bitterly that he had not encountered this delectable dish before. Now . . . (and a shameful thought crossed his mind) what New Zealand friends had he?

Among the solicitations in the Personal column, "Designing woman requires interesting assignments . . ." H'm. And what was this? "Old type rocking horses wanted. Condition unimportant." As if anyone in their right mind could possibly part with such a possession. He was reminded of his beloved Nelson, given to him on his fourth birthday, later enjoyed by his nephews and now by his great nephews. What a sterling steed he had been! Admittedly his trappings had become sadly perished through the years, but the heart of him was as sound as ever and his motion as steady. They are not made like that any more. He closed his eyes and slowly the paper slipped from his grasp.

At Cambridge he awoke unrefreshed. A sense of utter fatigue

had overtaken him and all movement now became a labour. Yet he had always enjoyed the act of arriving, a pleasure he was unwilling to forgo. So, to compensate for his low spirits, he commissioned his taxi to drive by way of Fen Causeway and along The Backs so that he could once more enjoy the flower gardens behind the colleges and the trim grasslands of the Granta riverbanks with their graceful willows. Here was serenity. Why, he wondered, should he ever again feel the need to set forth for distant parts. Here was peace; peace conducive to the fulfilment of his latest plan which was to write little essays on the times he had lived in.

He left his luggage at the outer gate of St Nicholas's College and paid off his taxi. As he approached the towered gateway at the end of the Long Walk, he could hear Dr Courtney's children at play in the Master's garden. Mr Jump, the head porter, was on duty at the Lodge and, after an exchange of civilities, 'I'll get Tom to take your luggage round right away,' said Mr Jump.

Davie walked on through the massive arch, across First Court and into Baxter's Court. The walk to M staircase seemed interminable. But here he was at his rooms—home at last. The familiar scene welcomed him: the letters set out on the table in orderly fashion by Mrs Tibbs, the bedmaker; Letty, the Rockingham Cow, on her bookcase gaping amiably across at the Boys Playing Marbles on the mantelpiece.

In a moment he would make a reviving pot of tea. But he was so extraordinarily tired as to be incapable of the immediate effort. He fell heavily into his armchair but felt unable to stir again. He would rest now. Secretly, peacefully he crossed the frontiers of sleep.

THE PERENNIAL LIBRARY MYSTERY SERIES

Delano Ames

CORPSE DIPLOMATIQUE   P 637, $2.84

"Sprightly and intelligent."

—*New York Herald Tribune Book Review*

FOR OLD CRIME'S SAKE   P 629, $2.84

MURDER, MAESTRO, PLEASE   P 630, $2.84

"If there is a more engaging couple in modern fiction than Jane and
Dagobert Brown, we have not met them."   —*Scotsman*

SHE SHALL HAVE MURDER   P 638, $2.84

"Combines the merit of both the English and American schools in the
new mystery. It's as breezy as the best of the American ones, and has
the sophistication and wit of any top-notch Britisher."

—*New York Herald Tribune Book Review*

E. C. Bentley

TRENT'S LAST CASE   P 440, $2.50

"One of the three best detective stories ever written."

—Agatha Christie

TRENT'S OWN CASE   P 516, $2.25

"I won't waste time saying that the plot is sound and the detection
satisfying. Trent has not altered a scrap and reappears with all his old
humor and charm."   —Dorothy L. Sayers

Gavin Black

A DRAGON FOR CHRISTMAS   P 473, $1.95

"Potent excitement!"   —*New York Herald Tribune*

THE EYES AROUND ME   P 485, $1.95

"I stayed up until all hours last night reading *The Eyes Around Me*,
which is something I do not do very often, but I was so intrigued by the
ingeniousness of Mr. Black's plotting and the witty way in which he spins
his mystery. I can only say that I enjoyed the book enormously."

—F. van Wyck Mason

YOU WANT TO DIE, JOHNNY?   P 472, $1.95

"Gavin Black doesn't just develop a pressure plot in suspense, he adds
uninfected wit, character, charm, and sharp knowledge of the Far East
to make rereading as keen as the first race-through."   —*Book Week*

Nicholas Blake

THE CORPSE IN THE SNOWMAN   P 427, $1.95
"If there is a distinction between the novel and the detective story (which we do not admit), then this book deserves a high place in both categories."   —*The New York Times*

THE DREADFUL HOLLOW   P 493, $1.95
"Pace unhurried, characters excellent, reasoning solid."
                    —*San Francisco Chronicle*

END OF CHAPTER   P 397, $1.95
". . . admirably solid . . . an adroit formal detective puzzle backed up by firm characterization and a knowing picture of London publishing."
                    —*The New York Times*

HEAD OF A TRAVELER   P 398, $2.25
"Another grade A detective story of the right old jigsaw persuasion."
                    —*New York Herald Tribune Book Review*

MINUTE FOR MURDER   P 419, $1.95
"An outstanding mystery novel. Mr. Blake's writing is a delight in itself."   —*The New York Times*

THE MORNING AFTER DEATH   P 520, $1.95
"One of Blake's best."   —Rex Warner

A PENKNIFE IN MY HEART   P 521, $2.25
"Style brilliant . . . and suspenseful."   —*San Francisco Chronicle*

THE PRIVATE WOUND   P 531, $2.25
[Blake's] best novel in a dozen years . . . . An intensely penetrating study of sexual passion. . . . A powerful story of murder and its aftermath."
                    —Anthony Boucher, *The New York Times*

A QUESTION OF PROOF   P 494, $1.95
"The characters in this story are unusually well drawn, and the suspense is well sustained."   —*The New York Times*

THE SAD VARIETY   P 495, $2.25
"It is a stunner. I read it instead of eating, instead of sleeping."
                    —Dorothy Salisbury Davis

THERE'S TROUBLE BREWING   P 569, $3.37
"Nigel Strangeways is a puzzling mixture of simplicity and penetration, but all the more real for that."   —*The Times Literary Supplement*

Nicholas Blake (cont'd)

THOU SHELL OF DEATH   P 428, $1.95

"It has all the virtues of culture, intelligence and sensibility that the most exacting connoisseur could ask of detective fiction."

—*The Times* [London] *Literary Supplement*

THE WIDOW'S CRUISE   P 399, $2.25

"A stirring suspense. . . . The thrilling tale leaves nothing to be desired."

—*Springfield Republican*

THE WORM OF DEATH   P 400, $2.25

"It [The Worm of Death] is one of Blake's very best—and his best is better than almost anyone's."   —Louis Untermeyer

John & Emery Bonett

A BANNER FOR PEGASUS   P 554, $2.40

"A gem! Beautifully plotted and set. . . . Not only is the murder adroit and deserved, and the detection competent, but the love story is charming."   —Jacques Barzun and Wendell Hertig Taylor

DEAD LION   P 563, $2.40

"A clever plot, authentic background and interesting characters highly recommended this one."   —*New Republic*

Christianna Brand

GREEN FOR DANGER   P 551, $2.50

"You have to reach for the greatest of Great Names (Christie, Carr, Queen . . .) to find Brand's rivals in the devious subtleties of the trade."

—Anthony Boucher

TOUR DE FORCE   P 572, $2.40

"Complete with traps for the over-ingenious, a double-reverse surprise ending and a key clue planted so fairly and obviously that you completely overlook it. If that's your idea of perfect entertainment, then seize at once upon *Tour de Force.*"   —Anthony Boucher, *The New York Times*

James Byrom

OR BE HE DEAD   P 585, $2.84

"A very original tale . . . Well written and steadily entertaining."

—Jacques Barzun & Wendell Hertig Taylor, *A Catalogue of Crime*

Henry Calvin

IT'S DIFFERENT ABROAD   P 640, $2.84

"What is remarkable and delightful, Mr. Calvin imparts a flavor of satire to what he renovates and compels us to take straight."

—Jacques Barzun

Marjorie Carleton

VANISHED   P 559, $2.40

"Exceptional . . . a minor triumph."
—Jacques Barzun and Wendell Hertig Taylor, *A Catalogue of Crime*

George Harmon Coxe

MURDER WITH PICTURES   P 527, $2.25

"[Coxe] has hit the bull's-eye with his first shot."

—*The New York Times*

Edmund Crispin

BURIED FOR PLEASURE   P 506, $2.50

"Absolute and unalloyed delight."

—Anthony Boucher, *The New York Times*

Lionel Davidson

THE MENORAH MEN   P 592, $2.84

"Of his fellow thriller writers, only John Le Carré shows the same instinct for the viscera."   —*Chicago Tribune*

NIGHT OF WENCESLAS   P 595, $2.84

"A most ingenious thriller, so enriched with style, wit, and a sense of serious comedy that it all but transcends its kind."

—*The New Yorker*

THE ROSE OF TIBET   P 593, $2.84

"I hadn't realized how much I missed the genuine Adventure story . . . until I read *The Rose of Tibet*."   —Graham Greene

D. M. Devine

MY BROTHER'S KILLER   P 558, $2.40

"A most enjoyable crime story which I enjoyed reading down to the last moment."   —Agatha Christie

Kenneth Fearing

THE BIG CLOCK   P 500, $1.95
"It will be some time before chill-hungry clients meet again so rare a compound of irony, satire, and icy-fingered narrative. *The Big Clock* is . . . a psychothriller you won't put down."   —*Weekly Book Review*

Andrew Garve

THE ASHES OF LODA   P 430, $1.50
"Garve . . . embellishes a fine fast adventure story with a more credible picture of the U.S.S.R. than is offered in most thrillers."
                                   —*The New York Times Book Review*

THE CUCKOO LINE AFFAIR   P 451, $1.95
". . . an agreeable and ingenious piece of work."   —*The New Yorker*

A HERO FOR LEANDA   P 429, $1.50
"One can trust Mr. Garve to put a fresh twist to any situation, and the ending is really a lovely surprise."   —*The Manchester Guardian*

MURDER THROUGH THE LOOKING GLASS   P 449, $1.95
". . . refreshingly out-of-the-way and enjoyable . . . highly recommended to all comers."   —*Saturday Review*

NO TEARS FOR HILDA   P 441, $1.95
"It starts fine and finishes finer. I got behind on breathing watching Max get not only his man but his woman, too."   —*Rex Stout*

THE RIDDLE OF SAMSON   P 450, $1.95
"The story is an excellent one, the people are quite likable, and the writing is superior."   —*Springfield Republican*

Michael Gilbert

BLOOD AND JUDGMENT   P 446, $1.95
"Gilbert readers need scarcely be told that the characters all come alive at first sight, and that his surpassing talent for narration enhances any plot. . . . Don't miss."   —*San Francisco Chronicle*

THE BODY OF A GIRL   P 459, $1.95
"Does what a good mystery should do: open up into all kinds of ramifications, with untold menace behind the action. At the end, there is a bang-up climax, and it is a pleasure to see how skilfully Gilbert wraps everything up."   —*The New York Times Book Review*

Michael Gilbert (cont'd)

THE DANGER WITHIN P 448, $1.95

"Michael Gilbert has nicely combined some elements of the straight detective story with plenty of action, suspense, and adventure, to produce a superior thriller." —*Saturday Review*

FEAR TO TREAD P 458, $1.95

"Merits serious consideration as a work of art."

—*The New York Times*

Joe Gores

HAMMETT P 631, $2.84

"Joe Gores at his very best. Terse, powerful writing—with the master, Dashiell Hammett, as the protagonist in a novel I think he would have been proud to call his own." —Robert Ludlum

C. W. Grafton

BEYOND A REASONABLE DOUBT P 519, $1.95

"A very ingenious tale of murder . . . a brilliant and gripping narrative."
—Jacques Barzun and Wendell Hertig Taylor

THE RAT BEGAN TO GNAW THE ROPE P 639, $2.84

"Fast, humorous story with flashes of brilliance."

—*The New Yorker*

Edward Grierson

THE SECOND MAN P 528, $2.25

"One of the best trial-testimony books to have come along in quite a while." —*The New Yorker*

Bruce Hamilton

TOO MUCH OF WATER P 635, $2.84

"A superb sea mystery. . . . The prose is excellent."
—Jacques Barzun and Wendell Hertig Taylor, *A Catalogue of Crime*

Cyril Hare

DEATH IS NO SPORTSMAN P 555, $2.40

"You will be thrilled because it succeeds in placing an ingenious story in a new and refreshing setting. . . . The identity of the murderer is really a surprise." —*Daily Mirror*

Cyril Hare (cont'd)

DEATH WALKS THE WOODS   P 556, $2.40

"Here is a fine formal detective story, with a technically brilliant solution demanding the attention of all connoisseurs of construction."
—Anthony Boucher, *The New York Times Book Review*

AN ENGLISH MURDER   P 455, $2.50

"By a long shot, the best crime story I have read for a long time. Everything is traditional, but originality does not suffer. The setting is perfect. Full marks to Mr. Hare."   —*Irish Press*

SUICIDE EXCEPTED   P 636, $2.84

"Adroit in its manipulation . . . and distinguished by a plot-twister which I'll wager Christie wishes she'd thought of."
—*The New York Times*

TENANT FOR DEATH   P 570, $2.84

"The way in which an air of probability is combined both with clear, terse narrative and with a good deal of subtle suburban atmosphere, proves the extreme skill of the writer."   —*The Spectator*

TRAGEDY AT LAW   P 522, $2.25

"An extremely urbane and well-written detective story."
—*The New York Times*

UNTIMELY DEATH   P 514, $2.25

"The English detective story at its quiet best, meticulously underplayed, rich in perceivings of the droll human animal and ready at the last with a neat surprise which has been there all the while had we but wits to see it."   —*New York Herald Tribune Book Review*

THE WIND BLOWS DEATH   P 589, $2.84

"A plot compounded of musical knowledge, a Dickens allusion, and a subtle point in law is related with delightfully unobtrusive wit, warmth, and style."   —*The New York Times*

WITH A BARE BODKIN   P 523, $2.25

"One of the best detective stories published for a long time."
—*The Spectator*

Robert Harling

THE ENORMOUS SHADOW   P 545, $2.50

"In some ways the best spy story of the modern period. . . . The writing is terse and vivid . . . the ending full of action . . . altogether first-rate."
—Jacques Barzun and Wendell Hertig Taylor, *A Catalogue of Crime*

Matthew Head

THE CABINDA AFFAIR   P 541, $2.25
"An absorbing whodunit and a distinguished novel of atmosphere."
                                    —Anthony Boucher, *The New York Times*

THE CONGO VENUS   P 597, $2.84
"Terrific. The dialogue is just plain wonderful."
                                                    —*The Boston Globe*

MURDER AT THE FLEA CLUB   P 542, $2.50
"The true delight is in Head's style, its limpid ease combined with humor
and an awesome precision of phrase."   —*San Francisco Chronicle*

M. V. Heberden

ENGAGED TO MURDER   P 533, $2.25
"Smooth plotting."   —*The New York Times*

James Hilton

WAS IT MURDER?   P 501, $1.95
"The story is well planned and well written."
                                                    —*The New York Times*

P. M. Hubbard

HIGH TIDE   P 571, $2.40
"A smooth elaboration of mounting horror and danger."
                                                        —*Library Journal*

Elspeth Huxley

THE AFRICAN POISON MURDERS   P 540, $2.25
"Obscure venom, manical mutilations, deadly bush fire, thrilling climax
compose major opus.... Top-flight."
                                        —*Saturday Review of Literature*

MURDER ON SAFARI   P 587, $2.84
"Right now we'd call Mrs. Huxley a dangerous rival to Agatha Christie."   —*Books*

Francis Iles

BEFORE THE FACT P 517, $2.50

"Not many 'serious' novelists have produced character studies to compare with Iles's internally terrifying portrait of the murderer in *Before the Fact*, his masterpiece and a work truly deserving the appellation of unique and beyond price." —Howard Haycraft

MALICE AFORETHOUGHT P 532, $1.95

"It is a long time since I have read anything so good as *Malice Aforethought*, with its cynical humour, acute criminology, plausible detail and rapid movement. It makes you hug yourself with pleasure."
—H. C. Harwood, *Saturday Review*

Michael Innes

THE CASE OF THE JOURNEYING BOY P 632, $3.12

"I could see no faults in it. There is no one to compare with him."
—*Illustrated London News*

DEATH BY WATER P 574, $2.40

"The amount of ironic social criticism and deft characterization of scenes and people would serve another author for six books."
—Jacques Barzun and Wendell Hertig Taylor

HARE SITTING UP P 590, $2.84

"There is hardly anyone (in mysteries or mainstream) more exquisitely literate, allusive and Jamesian—and hardly anyone with a firmer sense of melodramatic plot or a more vigorous gift of storytelling."
—Anthony Boucher, *The New York Times*

THE LONG FAREWELL P 575, $2.40

"A model of the deft, classic detective story, told in the most wittily diverting prose." —*The New York Times*

THE MAN FROM THE SEA P 591, $2.84

"The pace is brisk, the adventures exciting and excitingly told, and above all he keeps to the very end the interesting ambiguity of the man from the sea." —*New Statesman*

THE SECRET VANGUARD P 584, $2.84

"Innes . . . has mastered the art of swift, exciting and well-organized narrative." —*The New York Times*

THE WEIGHT OF THE EVIDENCE P 633, $2.84

"First-class puzzle, deftly solved. University background interesting and amusing." —*Saturday Review of Literature*

Mary Kelly

THE SPOILT KILL   P 565, $2.40

"Mary Kelly is a new Dorothy Sayers. . . . [An] exciting new novel."
—*Evening News*

Lange Lewis

THE BIRTHDAY MURDER   P 518, $1.95

"Almost perfect in its playlike purity and delightful prose."
—Jacques Barzun and Wendell Hertig Taylor

Allan MacKinnon

HOUSE OF DARKNESS   P 582, $2.84

"His best . . . a perfect compendium."
—Jacques Barzun & Wendell Hertig Taylor, *A Catalogue of Crime*

Arthur Maling

LUCKY DEVIL   P 482, $1.95

"The plot unravels at a fast clip, the writing is breezy and Maling's
approach is as fresh as today's stockmarket quotes."
—*Louisville Courier Journal*

RIPOFF   P 483, $1.95

"A swiftly paced story of today's big business is larded with intrigue as
a Ralph Nader-type investigates an insurance scandal and is soon on the
run from a hired gun and his brother. . . . Engrossing and credible."
—*Booklist*

SCHROEDER'S GAME   P 484, $1.95

"As the title indicates, this Schroeder is up to something, and the un-
ravelling of his game is a diverting and sufficiently blood-soaked entertainment."   —*The New Yorker*

Austin Ripley

MINUTE MYSTERIES   P 387, $2.50

More than one hundred of the world's shortest detective stories. Only
one possible solution to each case!

Thomas Sterling

THE EVIL OF THE DAY   P 529, $2.50

"Prose as witty and subtle as it is sharp and clear. . .characters unconven-
tionally conceived and richly bodied forth . . . . In short, a novel to be
treasured."   —Anthony Boucher, *The New York Times*

Julian Symons

THE BELTING INHERITANCE   P 468, $1.95
"A superb whodunit in the best tradition of the detective story."
                                    —August Derleth, *Madison Capital Times*

BLAND BEGINNING   P 469, $1.95
"Mr. Symons displays a deft storytelling skill, a quiet and literate wit,
a nice feeling for character, and detectival ingenuity of a high order."
                                    —Anthony Boucher, *The New York Times*

BOGUE'S FORTUNE   P 481, $1.95
"There's a touch of the old sardonic humour, and more than a touch of
style."   —*The Spectator*

THE BROKEN PENNY   P 480, $1.95
"The most exciting, astonishing and believable spy story to appear in
years.   —Anthony Boucher, *The New York Times Book Review*

THE COLOR OF MURDER   P 461, $1.95
"A singularly unostentatious and memorably brilliant detective story."
                                    —*New York Herald Tribune Book Review*

Dorothy Stockbridge Tillet
(John Stephen Strange)

THE MAN WHO KILLED FORTESCUE   P 536, $2.25
"Better than average."   —*Saturday Review of Literature*

Simon Troy

THE ROAD TO RHUINE   P 583, $2.84
"Unusual and agreeably told."   —*San Francisco Chronicle*

SWIFT TO ITS CLOSE   P 546, $2.40
"A nicely literate British mystery . . . the atmosphere and the plot are
exceptionally well wrought, the dialogue excellent."   —*Best Sellers*

Henry Wade

THE DUKE OF YORK'S STEPS   P 588, $2.84
"A classic of the golden age."
  —Jacques Barzun & Wendell Hertig Taylor, *A Catalogue of Crime*

A DYING FALL   P 543, $2.50
"One of those expert British suspense jobs . . . it crackles with undercur-
rents of blackmail, violent passion and murder. Topnotch in its class."
                                                         —*Time*

Henry Wade (cont'd)

THE HANGING CAPTAIN   P 548, $2.50

"This is a detective story for connoisseurs, for those who value clear thinking and good writing above mere ingenuity and easy thrills."

—*Times Literary Supplement*

Hillary Waugh

LAST SEEN WEARING . . .   P 552, $2.40

"A brilliant tour de force."   —Julian Symons

THE MISSING MAN   P 553, $2.40

"The quiet detailed police work of Chief Fred C. Fellows, Stockford, Conn., is at its best in *The Missing Man* . . . one of the Chief's toughest cases and one of the best handled."

—Anthony Boucher, *The New York Times Book Review*

Henry Kitchell Webster

WHO IS THE NEXT?   P 539, $2.25

"A double murder, private-plane piloting, a neat impersonation, and a delicate courtship are adroitly combined by a writer who knows how to use the language."   —Jacques Barzun and Wendell Hertig Taylor

Anna Mary Wells

MURDERER'S CHOICE   P 534, $2.50

"Good writing, ample action, and excellent character work."

—*Saturday Review of Literature*

A TALENT FOR MURDER   P 535, $2.25

"The discovery of the villain is a decided shock."   —*Books*

Edward Young

THE FIFTH PASSENGER   P 544, $2.25

"Clever and adroit . . . excellent thriller . . ."   —*Library Journal*

If you enjoyed this book you'll want to know about
THE PERENNIAL LIBRARY MYSTERY SERIES

Buy them at your local bookstore or use this coupon for ordering:

Qty	P number	Price
	postage and handling charge	$1.00
	_____ book(s) @ $0.25	
	TOTAL	

Prices contained in this coupon are Harper & Row invoice prices only. They are subject to change without notice, and in no way reflect the prices at which these books may be sold by other suppliers.

HARPER & ROW, Mail Order Dept. #PMS, 10 East 53rd St., New York, N.Y. 10022.

Please send me the books I have checked above. I am enclosing $_____ which includes a postage and handling charge of $1.00 for the first book and 25¢ for each additional book. Send check or money order. No cash or C.O.D.s please

Name_____

Address_____

City_____State_____Zip_____

Please allow 4 weeks for delivery. USA only. This offer expires 3/31/85.
Please add applicable sales tax.